Issue 2

EDITED BY:
Ianna A. Small

midnight & indigo
PUBLISHING

midnight & indigo

VOLUME 1, ISSUE 2
 ISBN 978-1-7328917-2-2

midnightandindigo.com

———————

MANUSCRIPTS AND SUBMISSIONS
Whether you've already been published or are just starting out, we want to hear from you! We accept submissions of short stories and narrative essays written by Black women writers. View complete submission guidelines and submit your stories online at *midnightandindigo.com*. No paper submissions please.

Cover image: BONNINSTUDIO/Stocksy United

Printed and bound in the United States of America.
First Printing October 2019

midnight & indigo humbly acknowledges the support of the following writers. Thank you for lending your words and stories to our platforms and for trusting us with your voices:

Aretha Abrams
Biba Adams
Muli Amaye
Nikita Anderson
Maya Angelique
Jacquese Armstrong
Khaholi Bailey
Zakiah Baker
DeMisty Bellinger
L.M. Bennett
Christine Jean Blain
rebekah blake
Kenia Burke
K.B. Carle
Yolande Clark-Jackson
Jeannine A. Cook
Tracy Cross
Elizabeth Crowder
Joi Donaldson
Cassandra Eddington
Desiree Evans
Adina Ferguson
Johannah Fienburgh
Ebony Frier
Wandeka Gayle
JaQuette Gilbert
Janyce Denise Glasper
Ciana Hamilton
Azuree Harrison
Avi-Yona Israel
Candace Jozef
Cierra Kaler-Jones
Njera Keith
Tahirah Lawrence

Marissa Leotaud
Candice Lola
devorah major
DiAnne Malone
Maria Elena Montero
Lauren Morton
Latanya Muhammad
Onicia Muller
Ilisha Nicole
Theresa Okokon
Jackie Oldham
Sierra Paige
Ashley Paul
Tzynya Pinchback
Choya Randolph
Mary Retta
Kourtnie Rodney
Jeanna Rutledge
Zuri H. Scrivens
Malayka Small
Jeannette Smith
Sylvannia Soulet
Theresa Sylvester
Tia Swain
Tatiana Taylor
Vanessa Taylor
Maria Thompson Corley
Charissa Townsend
Sekai Ward
Rehshetta Wells
Brianna Wheeler
Janelle M. Williams
Preslaysa Williams
Akilah Wise

*"I'm a believer in the power of knowledge and the ferocity of beauty,
so from my point of view, your life is already artful -
waiting, just waiting, for you to make it art."*

Toni Morrison
Rest In Peace

midnight
&indigo
celebrating black women writers

ISSUE 2

IANNA A. SMALL

Editor's Note

The past few months have been a whirlwind; complete with the blessing of an overabundance of new stories, written and conceived, and anxiety about the realization of a dream coming to pass. The feedback from our inaugural issue has truly been humbling.

With confirmation of the space for our stories in this corner of literature, I'm excited to share a second collection with you. Thank you so much for your support.

In this issue, we present new works by fourteen Black women storytellers; introducing a diverse array of characters, ranging from a girl anxious to understand the goings-on, on the other side of a window, to a middle-aged man content to view the world from his porch - until he isn't. We explore the awkwardness of love; romantic, familial, and unrequited, and even grapple with the validity of memories and the choices we make that often yield unexpected results.

In **"Wick"** by K.B. Carle, the windows of the Big House separate Sylke from the house slave she visits at night. She can't help but wonder what this woman feels while she tends to the Master's family, and why she allows the drippings of candle wax to seep into the palm of her hand.

A young woman hides her love for her best friend, who is currently dating someone else in **"Crazy"** by Marissa Joy Leotaud. One of them decides to finally reveal their true feelings.

An old woman, who appears to be homeless, encounters a couple on a train and tells them the story of her searching in **"Sunday"** by Cassandra Eddington.

In **"Kelsey Monahan Stole Your Goddamn Jacket"** by Vanessa Taylor, a narrator returns to a shelter to find their roommate has stolen their jacket. In this story that touches on homelessness, shelter life, queerness, and Islam, what is otherwise a mundane event leads to an explosive reaction.

"The Goodbye Sister" by Janyce Denise Glasper introduces an

Ohioan woman coming to terms with the absence of her younger sister. One sister continually returns to the insufferable misery, while the other is quick to flee and never return.

A Black woman is annoyed by the poor customer service at her local Harlem Post Office, in **"In c/o Chidi Onyeachu"** by Janelle M. Williams. In line, she obsesses over her ex-boyfriend, to whom she is sending a package that is literally stabbing her. Upon revealing that the package contains her heart, everyone has an opinion.

In **"Sitting Spells"** by devorah major, Meecha makes a real love potion. She sends every young woman who seeks her help, to her sister Rhea for her cautionary tale about the truth of these potions. Are they worth it?

"Up North" by Zakiah Baker follows a young girl through her 1950s summer journey of moving from a poverty-stricken South Carolina town to a wealthy city in Pennsylvania. When she meets free-spirited Cindy, she wonders whether she could be more than what she's been taught.

A mother and daughter come to terms with their mortality at different points in their lives in **"Mary, Mara, and Death"** by rebekah blake.

Jamie recalls the night his little sister was born, in **"Pomegranate"** by Johannah Fienburgh. It was a night of fairy tales, power outages, and strange fruits fed to him by his mother. Jamie wonders what is memory and what is story.

In **"Mr. Landry"** by Akilah Wise, Mr. Landry spends his days watching the world from his porch in rural Louisiana. As the day turns to night on one particular day, he encounters a wide-eyed local who sparks a peculiar kind of fire.

Black Barbie, a personal essay by Khaholi Bailey, recounts her experience at the slumber party of a fellow fourth-grader, and the regift of one of her unopened toys: a Black Barbie doll. Latent racism, inferiority, and white guilt are revealed.

Little Brother by Zuri H. Scrivens was written following the news that one of her maternal uncles had died. The essay draws on her memories of the first time she heard her mother grieve, and how it shifted the concept of her familial role.

Lastly, *We Are The Champions* by Jeannine A. Cook, describes a trip to an abortion clinic, taking the reader on the mental journey to an internal war. On the other side, we recognize how many other women warriors are fighting beside us to overcome similar battles.

If you're interested in reading additional stories by Black women writers, please don't forget to visit us online at midnightandindigo.com and follow us on social media @midnightandindigo.

Enjoy!

Ianna

Wick

A woman Sylke calls Wick leaves etchings of her lips on the Master's windows while catching the drippings of candles in the palm of her hand. Sylke finds her in the quiet of the nighttime, watches her drift through the Big House from her settling branch on a big tree, willow leaves keeping her small body to themselves. Mantis tickles her scalp with her claws, scraping at dirt bits and whatever else she finds.

Unlike Sylke, Mantis has no interest in the woman who dances in the smoke trails of candlelight.

Sylke's mama, Abigail, tells her that everyone and everything has a name. That those working in the Big House probably have day names that sound like bird songs or the gentle humming of bees. From her gazing spot, Sylke releases her day name, Barbaidy, into the air. Listens for the hummings or songs it might sing but only hears Mantis whisper, *Sylke.*

A name made special, one Sylke can hold or give to the ones that fill her with a warmth she frees when she's scared. A reminder that she is more than just Barbaidy, a name made for Master Laide that burns and causes her tongue to get to tangling, forming new shapes that threaten to choke her.

Sylke doesn't keep too many names in her mind and knows it's not her place to give Wick a birthing name. But everyone and everything has a name, and though *Wick* may not hum, it's something Sylke can settle on, feeling closer to the woman in the window.

Wick appears next to Young Master Laide, candle making the room glow so Sylke can see inside. She likes to think Wick does this just for her. Tiny horses form rows on the floor, all trying to escape between Wick's legs and out the door. Papers with black lines and spots of blue and green cover the walls, something Sylke can't get her mind to hold on to but wonders if those are the places horses dream of going. She flicks Mantis to distract her thoughts from getting caught up in things she can't make sense of from a branch. Mantis pulls on a single strand of Sylke's hair, a warning prick to be still.

Wick moves closer to Young Master Laide, slides a finger under his nose. Pulls the covers up until his feet show, toes squirming around each other. He sleeps, even while Wick presses the back of her hand against his cheek. Moves his hair from his forehead.

Tips her candle over his open mouth, watching the wax fall.

Even Mantis stills to watch.

Something stirs behind her, causes Wick to catch the wax in the palm of her hand, curl her fingers around the small pool in her palm. Mistress Laide is in the doorway, blonde hair reminding Sylke of spider web threads. They switch places, Mistress Laide sitting on the edge of her son's bed. Sylke knows about the Mistress' wandering soul. How, in the night, she drifts with no place to rest, all the thoughts that keep her feet stirring coming up all at once.

"Where does her soul wander?" Sylke imagines asking Wick, whose hand drags along Young Master Laide's doorframe, wax flakes disappearing in the dark.

If Mantis has any answers, she keeps them to herself.

The flame bends when Wick finds Master Laide, scribbling and drinking something Sylke can't see. She assumes it's the drink that makes Master Laide's cheeks swell, turn red, and gives him the sweats. The stuff he loses his words to and laughs when he trips over people he sees but no one else can.

Sylke thinks the flame is trying to pull away. Same way she does when Master Laide wanders onto the pebble trail passing between slave cabins, drinking, yelling, and laughing.

All while glass shards dig into the one he blames for tripping him.

Tries to pull away like Wick does when Master Laide grips her wrist, lips pecking her neck while his hand disappears somewhere in her dress. And Wick stands, lips curling in on themselves, letting the flame curl around the trembling fingers of her free hand.

Master Laide releases her, holds his glass for Wick to fill. For the first time, she leaves her candle behind. Sylke thinks she looks small without its light. Skin the color of the wicker basket Mistress Laide has Sylke collect flowers in. Same flowers wasps like to curl in, always waiting for someone to trick into a fight.

Only wasps speak in challenges and needle stings instead of whisperings.

Sylke pulls herself closer to the edge of her settling branch, feels the bark scrape her legs. She doesn't want the flame to go away, for everything on the other side of the glass to be lost. Despite Mantis tapping on her forehead, she slides forward, wanting more of Wick. Of what Wick sees. Of what Wick feels when the wax seeps into her skin.

But Wick is standing there, facing Sylke with her palm pressing on the glass. Sylke reaches for her, the tips of their fingers meeting against the cold glass. She imagines what Wick's skin feels like as they stare at each other, eyes tracing over their hands, eyes, and face. Holding on to each other even while a shadow grows behind Wick.

Mantis flies between them.

Away.

Sylke hears the humming, faint but it's there if she closes her eyes, calms her breath. She opens them in time to see Wick pull her hand away, lips sharing words Sylke can't hear.

Mantis flies into Sylke's forehead until she slips away from the cool glass of windows holding all the things her mind can't settle on but wants to hold all at once.

From Master Laide and the crooked smile that grows when he passes the candle to a woman she calls Wick.

Who leaves etchings of her lips on the Master's windows.

While catching the drippings of candles in the palm of her hand.

Crazy

Two sticks of incense burn. Tufts of smoke waft through the air, rising and curling, swelling then evaporating like pulsing thoughts that remain secret; drifting off before full expression, leaving only their fragrance behind. One stick lavender, the other cedarwood. Familiar, comforting scents.

We met back in college, the only Black students in our American literature class. He gave me the Black person head nod of acknowledgment. I nodded in his direction politely, and we silently addressed each other's presence in front of the whites. Internally, we screamed, "Thank God you're here! Sit next to me!"

We sat next to each other.

I got him cedarwood incense that first Christmas. Neither of us could afford to fly home.

I've been buying him the sweet-smelling sticks ever since.

Five years later and I'm with him again on Christmas. Still too broke to go home. It's okay. His loft is home enough.

His girlfriend comes from money. Goes home every year. I stay here with him, not overnight, just on Christmas Day. It worries her all the same.

"It drives her crazy," he tells me.

"Why don't you go with her?"

"Can't afford it. And I'd never let them pay."

He'd never let them pay.

He's a beautiful, Black, renaissance man. The Darius Lovehall to my Nina Mosley, although I'm no Nina Mosley. He wears mustard-colored beanies and thrift store jeans, and jackets that used to be his grandfather's. He listens to nothing but jazz. Coltrane's "Giant Steps" in heavy rotation. He doesn't eat meat but doesn't judge me when I do. If he were white, he'd be a thorn in the side, an appropriator of culture. But he's a Black man and everything that comes with it. His liberal nature is a triumph over Sundays in pews seated under the boom of sweaty, judgmental pastors; his father's voice telling him to be a man, his mother's telling him to pull up his pants, cut off his dreads, and assimilate with a smile.

His liberal nature is pride, strength, and bravery in the face of police and nervous white women. His record collection, his love for Ethiopian food and James Baldwin, a celebration of those who paved the way for him. He is no appropriator of culture.

He's a beautiful Black renaissance man, the Darius Lovehall to my Nina Mosley, although I'm no Nina Mosley. I'm a filmmaker who tells the same story over and over. A sheltered girl who breaks free, finds her voice, her sexual presence. I'm not well-read. I know of classic Hollywood films and a handful of Italian cinematic masterpieces, but I can't quote Baldwin and I can't stand jazz. It doesn't sound too bad here, though. Here in his loft with its exposed beams and brick walls. If his rent wasn't fixed sophomore year, he wouldn't be able to afford this place now. The space is meant for him. I am meant to stand here and watch him, breathe him in, be his best friend.

"Look at this," he says.

He takes me by the hand and pulls me over to the solid mahogany table planted in the center of the room. It's sheet music. He's a musician that writes his own. I love it when he plays his keyboard or feebly attempts the saxophone. I never tell him how much.

"I'm no Coltrane," he says.

I can only assume as much. I'm the last person who'd know.

"You know I can't read music," I say.

"Yeah, but isn't it beautiful?"

"It's pretty to look at."

"It's called 'Bear'. It's your Christmas present."

"It's for me?"

His nickname for me is Bear.

"Merry Christmas," he says.

"You do things like this, and that's why your girlfriend gets nervous with me around."

I am playful, give him a push on the arm, and refuse to show him how he has moved me with my new favorite song that I've never heard. He laughs a small laugh, a curt puff of air escaping his nostrils. He shakes his head but says nothing more as his gaze follows out the window.

He's probably thinking I'm crazy to worry. His girlfriend is crazy to worry. I'm no threat. She should know that the way he knows it.

"Thank you," I say.

"Don't thank me yet. Let me play it for you."

He pulls out his keyboard, stumbles through at first then falls into a rhythm. It's a simple tune, slow and romantic, or maybe I just think so.

It starts to snow outside. He finishes the song then turns up the heat. He knows I get cold.

"Well, what do you think? Do you like it? How does it make you feel?"

He asks not to gauge my emotion, but his talent.

"Crazy," I say. "I feel crazy."

He comes close to me. Stands directly in front of me and presses one hand on the center of my chest. He feels the frantic heartbeat I'm constantly attempting to hide when I'm with him. An orchestra playing below my sternum. The swell of the bass, the vibrations of the cello, the sweetness of violins fluttering up from my belly.

He feels it all.

"Crazy?" I ask her. "Why crazy?"

She takes a breath and I keep my hand where it is, let it rise and fall with her chest.

"What are you doing?" she asks.

"I want to feel your heart when I tell you this."

My forehead falls into place against hers. We look down at the sliver of space between us, the sliver that holds the possibilities we do not indulge, the lines we do not cross.

"Well, go on."

"I don't have a girlfriend."

"What do you mean?"

"As of this morning, I don't."

She breathes. "What happened?"

"She told me she couldn't date a man who loves another woman."

She breathes deeper.

"And she's right," I say. "She shouldn't have to do that."

She was my lady for two years. When we started dating, I needed to move on from the relationship trapped in my heart, the relationship

I knew I'd never have with Bear.

Bear is my best friend, and I know I'd be a fool to lose that. I'd be a fool to sacrifice the one person who never judged, never betrayed, never left. Some jars fill up on their own, overflow when you're not paying attention. And the next thing you know, you can't help it, there's water all over the floor and you're in love. You slip and slide and pretend you have balance, but you're a fool on your ass and everyone can see it.

The girlfriend's parents never offered to fly me to their Connecticut home. I didn't need them to. I was taught to save, live below my means. It is the only lie I told, besides withholding my love, the story that I had to stay here with her because I couldn't afford to travel to my significant other's home. I couldn't tell her the truth without the risk of losing her. A risk I was never willing to take.

Bear isn't a cool girl. She doesn't pretend to like what I like. She drinks wine instead of whiskey. She speaks film while I speak tunes. She doesn't act like she couldn't care less while caring too much about what I think. She rarely agrees with me and always tells me when I'm wrong. I listen because I trust her and know her words come with love. Could it be love? Not just her thoughtful dialogues, her gentle criticisms, but all of it. How she feels about all of me.

I can be over confident. Women loving me is nothing new, but a cocky man is the first to fall. My mother warns me of that and I take heed.

Perhaps Bear loves me like she loves her little brother, a college freshman starting to find his way, in constant need of advice. Perhaps she loves me like the baby she lost. Fathered by a fool who wanted no part, the baby slipping on to the next life before becoming a part of this one. I held her for three days while she wept, and she didn't stop me when I stroked her hair. Didn't argue with me when I told her she'd be all right.

She's the Nina Mosley to my Darius Lovehall, although I'm no Darius Lovehall. She's my forever muse. My uncontrollable source of desire despite conflicting expectations, communication, or my ego.

She's a filmmaker, raw and vulnerable. Her stories have no filter, sort of like her heart. She's smart and expressive and sexy and, my God, I think she barely knows it. She is more than what's ever been desired, the Nina Mosley to my Darius Lovehall, although I'm no Darius Lovehall. I'm a man who admires the art of others but struggles to create his own. Perhaps because most of my passion lies in a concealed chamber of my heart.

I've known it, her beauty, since I was a boy, seventeen but ahead in school, starting my first year in college. I nodded at her, acknowledging the presence of another in the sea of white faces. But I knew there was more to her beauty, even then. I knew I wanted it to be more, wanted her to be special. I wasn't prepared to handle her greatness at the time.

I dated. She dated. We stayed Black student allies, confidants, and friends.

I didn't want to be her friend.

Our heads still touch, my hand still on her heart, we start to sway. Try to soothe the rising tension like a baby that needs to be put to bed.

She clears her throat slightly. "Who is it...that you're in love with?"

I hold those final precious moments of my secret and wish she could feel how rapidly my own heart beats.

I clear my throat, but it barely makes a sound. The moment has arrived. I've held out a hand, an invitation to wade in the water, but I can't seem to make the final plunge or tell her the water is fine. Words scramble in my mind, lodge in my throat.

She is patient with me. Puts a hand on my back and leads our sway.

Coltrane swells on the stereo, playing the notes I wish I could say.

"Tell me something," she says.

"What do you want to hear? An allegory about two ships passing in the night? Maybe a story of a lost man with a compass in his pocket. Don't you see? You and me, we are the allegory."

The lavender smoke dances its body around the cedarwood flame. The fragrances rise, swell, and evaporate together.

We sway.

Sunday

I.

They walk into the train car and toward the empty seats across from me, see me, stutter as they sit down. It does not bother me, I am patient. They avoid looking at me. To them, it is more polite that they pretend I am not here. I wait.

I see the sadness in her eyes, the glistening, the gentle tension in her eyebrows. I am unfortunate. I am a victim of something. It pains her young mind to think of what, so she makes a wall with her furrowing.

He crosses his hands in his lap. He examines his knuckles, the crescent-shaped scar from the lid of a can. It has healed wide at the center. His face is tilted in the way that heads tilt to honor God. He clears his throat. He adjusts the angle of his sneakers, the distance between his knees.

I look to my reflection in the window between their heads. I am old. I have aged again, the deep downward scratches in the glass intersect with the lines beneath my eyes. There are three now, deep and brown. A mole rides the ridge of the third fold beneath my left eye. I put one finger to it.

He puts his hand on her knee.

II.

I see small toes wriggling, grains of sand collected beneath white crescent nails. I watch foam cover my toes and then recede. My feet sink.

Quicksand, I think.

A cartoon clip of a coyote descending, body stiff and eyes wide, plays out in my head. I giggle.

The sun is overhead like an egg cracked open into the sky, yellow yolk melting down over my head. The warmth of it covers my shoulders, and I shiver with pleasure.

I take a step forward. I watch the moisture leave the spot that bears my weight. Like a drum beat, like a rock dropping, it radiates out from the center moving away from me.

I am a child. Everything is something else. I am making connections; this thing is like that, that thing is like this. The world becomes an endless loop of meaning that I am trying to tap into with my likenings. I am so small in this moment that I can only feel wonder. It is my very first time. The ocean, a vast blanket of water so close to my home, but I am only now visiting it at the age of six. Curiosity pushes me forward, a step more. The tide returns, water up to my ankles this time, then pulls away and back into the deep. Foam sits on the slopes of my feet. *Pop pop*, small bubbles departing. It almost tickles. Between the tingling of my shoulders and scalp and the tickling of my feet, I am in ecstasy. I have never felt such deep satisfaction.

From the boardwalk, I hear my mother's voice calling, Return. So many rumors about what is in the water. Purity. There is no purity left in the world, she says.

It takes every ounce of my obedience to listen to her.

As I grow, I hold this memory. There is no experience that has supplanted this one. I become anxious with the desire, and I beg my mother to take me back to the ocean. She does so reluctantly, but tells me that I can only stand there. I am not to go in. And so I repeat this edging carefully each time, each Sunday when I run the two blocks from the church to the pier, from the pier to the ocean, and stand waiting for my mother to say, Return.

As the years pass, I am excellent in school, a star pupil. Perfect attendance, perfect behavior, perfect grades. There is no way in which I am lacking, and my mother's pride is clear from the way she beams at me over the edge of my blue report card, the cardstock stiff in her hand. She adds the news to the church announcements and the old ladies in their ornate hats clap for me and pinch my cheeks and give me an extra-large slice of cake after the service. I learn from them, swiftly, how I ought to be in the world and this lesson sticks with me through my fifth-grade graduation, my hair in two bobbled twists hanging thickly from the crown of my head. Pink and yellow dress. It was always one of my favorites. I wore it until it was so tight that it ripped beneath the left armpit when I went to reach for the milk from the fridge.

In middle school I am a star again, but school begins to bore me. So I try to make the other students laugh when I am done with my work early and waiting for the teacher to move us onto the next task. My marks in behavior begin to suffer.

I spend my free time pushing the boundaries of my younger years. I see the tire of my bicycle threading the yellow line in the center of the street. It is Saturday, listless. The hot sun beams overhead. I ride through the neighborhood to pick up Angie on my pegs. I tell her stories. They are mostly stories about a world that I inhabit, all my own, or sea creatures and woodland creatures that can talk. Angie and I have never seen the woods. Where we live, there are grids of houses and old shop buildings and the newer, larger buildings that are popping up every day now. The closest we have come to the wild is the overgrown lot of weeds two blocks east of my house and the field mice and stray cats that live there.

I drop Angie off at home when she begins to protest that we are riding too far and I set out again for the edges of the boundary that my mother has set for me. I wander the aisles of the new Stop & Shop peppered with sand, looking at little cakes so preserved they hold their shape when I drop them on the sidewalk later. I stand beside the wreckage and watch the trains roll in from Manhattan. It's a new destination, the Rockaways. The city slickers pace the concrete while they squint in all directions.

Where? they ask.

This way? they squint.

Disoriented. Can't sense the water, can't see beyond a block. Too much sky, probably.

Some days they wander down my street and I point them in the right direction. I flick clods of dirt off of my porch while I wait for dinner.

This is where I'm sitting when I first see them, the line of them. Some heads are shaved, others are not, but they are all modestly clothed, wearing socks with their sandals and some holding blankets wrapped around their shoulders. They walk slowly, each moving at their own pace, steps out of sync, eyes fixed ahead of them but almost unseeing. They head south, toward the piers. They move so slowly that a small boy on the porch beside mine cries when he sees them and rushes inside. They are white, of course. Except for one of the two at the front of the line, one of her hands wrapped around the fist of the other at the base of her back. The line is following them. The woman in a bold maroon robe, the man in a rich orange. It is the color that catches my eye. My imagination is taken by the deep red maroon and the burning yellow-orange like the colors of an Indian blanket bloom parsed and saturated into cloth.

After they appear, they become a fixture. Every day they walk and the church ladies start to notice, coming home from work, peering out from their kitchens. They can't say why, but they are taken aback, offended. I think, with some wisdom beyond my years, that they are afraid. These people have taken up residence in the old Robinson house. They keep a chicken in their yard and spend hours sitting still. They can be seen plainly through the open windows. I spend years watching them.

III.

I see my mother baring her large white teeth. She is grimacing in a pink church suit at the door of my room. The collar hides her neck. She is standing beside a poster of a blue butterfly. I am sweating in my tank top. The air conditioner is broken.

She asks if I plan to shave my head. She tells me I can't come back if I do.

She tells me she is worried about my soul.

She asks, And what do those people say about hell?

I tell her that I don't know if I believe in all that.

She holds one hand to the tiny gold cross at her neck.

Didn't I raise you right?

We eat dinner in silence. At the end of the meal, she brings out a small birthday cake, the eighteen candles already lit, the light beneath her chin making her face look like a skull. She places the cake in front of me and sits silently. As the wax melts down, I lean in to blow out the candles. Swiftly, she leans in and extinguishes them with one deep exhale.

She leaves the table without saying a word. The next morning I leave with one bag over my shoulder.

IV.

I can see the Venerable Pema sitting in front of me. Her small round face, speckled. Black people spots. I think of Mama Dear, how she taught me to call them, pointing to the ridges of her own cheekbones. The Venerable Pema is covered in them. Spots on her face like a full moon, spots on what skin of her neck is visible. Such a nice color the rusty wise red of her robe, covering half a spot here, half a spot there.

A deep breath in through my nostrils and I listen as it echoes deep in the chambers of my ears, plugged up by orange bits of foam. Legs folded, skinny thighs stick to the foam of the yoga mat, tailbone balanced on a purple cushion, spine like iron.

I close my eyes.

I must concentrate. On the wave, the waves, the rising of one shape beside another. Phenomena. All water at the end, all atoms, all the same. What is a mango but a slightly different expression than that which makes an orange?

I picture the faces of the others sitting around me, my first friends away from home. Amy, Robert, Nico. We are one. I am happy here.

A deep breath.

I am a mango I am an orange I am a wave.

No such thing as purity.

This place was a deep comfort to me. I felt that I had found answers in these non answers to questions that I hadn't been asking. Who can sum up such an experience in adequate words? The only one who knows what those first few years did for me is the one who has done it too. Let it suffice to say that I touched something of what I had unwittingly been looking for. I would call those some of my most satisfied years. My time there came to a close too quickly. And, of course, I can say that looking back, had I known then what I know now, I might have chosen to stay. But it only took once, the first time it ever happened, to throw me from that womb.

I heard a tone through the foam earplugs, and my fingers dug the bits out of my ears. I remember how it ached, their leaving. Sore. I twirled a pinky in my ear. The tips of the foam cones expanded as I picked small strings of earwax from them and rolled the wax into balls between my fingertips.

Pema smiled. She opened her mouth to add a thought and out flowed the rounded drawl of a Southern preacher, the Baptist church still in the cadence of her voice. I was comforted. The tales of a woman who walked her congregation from the doors of her church to the doors of another and left them. Sunday's orphans. She never looked back. She was the first to show me that we must all follow our own path. She was the first to tell me that my shame was not useful.

Pema spoke of the Buddha and I leaned back on my palms to listen. I lost track of Pema's voice as a thought occurred to me like the low hum of a single fly circling my head.

Cancer. Breast cancer.

I cocked my head sideways. I couldn't understand where the thought came from. Back then I thought, maybe I've read degeneracy in her posture, in the tone of her skin, the whites of her eyes. Maybe it was some subconscious measuring for which I couldn't consciously account.

I was lost in thought when the Venerable Pema stopped speaking and the others stood up to head to work hour. I swatted the thought away and headed out to the garden to pick tomatoes for supper. When I rolled out my cot on the top floor of the house, I had forgotten the thought, put it out of my head. But my dreams were dark and unintelligible, and when I woke I felt that a cloud had descended on me. I tried my best to sit with it, but the hours of meditation were hardly bearable, and I started to squirm where before a conscious effort wasn't even required to sit still.

During work hours, I wander the tall grass in the yard of the temple. I see it, just barely breathing, and I rush to take it in despite the memory of my mother's voice telling me to leave it. I swathe it in a kitchen towel, sit at the picnic tables along the fence, and hold it to my chest. An hour of small meows, small paws reaching. Another hour before it stops.

I look at my hands holding the runt of a litter. Kitten nose, kitten tail, kitten heart no longer beating. I feel more present than I have in any of the day's meditations and I think, no, no one can teach me out of the pain of small losses. And then, again, the fly is circling my head, the shadow of its body dozing around on the wood of the picnic table beneath me.

I couldn't concentrate. Eyes open, I watched the others as they meditated. They were too calm, too still. I imagined those faces lying down, arms crossed over their chests. My mind was playing tricks on me, trying to force the thought out of me. I see that now. Then, I simply wished that someone would open their eyes. It was snowing outside. The snow swirled and hovered before it descended. Like the snow, the fly circled, bounced. I tried to think of something else.

The bell marking the end of the meditation startled me. I watched the others leave the room, and the decision to stay felt like bravery that I had never summoned before. I crawled across the wooden floor and sat before her.

Teacher, I haven't been able to sleep.

What is troubling you?

Are you well?

The Venerable Pema says no. She has been to the doctor recently.

And so?

In this moment I felt that my heart was trying to escape me.

They are running some tests. Why do you ask?

The words tumbled from me, Breast cancer. Was it?

Pema is silent. Pema shifts.

How did you know?

After the conversation with Pema, I feel a sense of relief. My head is clear again and I sleep without dreams. I put the months of pain leading up to this conversation out of my mind, but I spend the days watching my Teacher carefully. She, too, is watching me carefully. When the tests come back positive, she asks me if there's anything else that she needs to know. I am taken aback by this belief in me, and it occurs to me for the first time that there is something to believe.

I tell her, simply, No. And I stay, learning from her until she stops teaching.

V.

The train jerks. I groan and sit up straight, rub my side with a stiff hand.

Ah! I take a deep breath, my lungs expanding, the vertebrae in my back suspended on stretching muscle, a gentle crackling warming the canal of my ear. I roll my neck once to hear a luscious pop, a shiver of pleasure over my back. I roll my ankle, warmth wriggles up my leg as the joints sound off.

I wonder if they can hear over the screeching rails of the train.

I cough longer than I intend to. This they can hear.

She wraps her arm around his, holding him against her body. She rests her head on the puffy blue shoulder of his coat. She closes her eyes. I see the skin between her eyes crinkle. She is thinking hard about me and trying not to.

She purses her lips.

Even with her eyes closed, she imagines my face as she has seen it out of the corner of her eye.

VI.

When the Venerable Pema dies, I cannot stop feeling such a deep degree of despair that all cessation of thought becomes impossible.

I try to sit through the pain, but I am fully aware of myself. I think of the months that preceded the conversation, I wonder what difference they may have made, and then I feel that my sense of responsibility is so absurd that I hate myself for assuming it. I must have seen it in her failing posture, in her eyes, in her hands. I must have made it all up.

Amy, too, is disparaged by the loss of our teacher.

Though I have shaved my head, I consider going home until she tells me about the Sufis living in the mountains north of the city. She talks to me about love, gratuitous, indulgent love, and her words seem so counter to everything that we've been taught that I immediately agree to accompany her.

VII.

I see Rabbia walking with the light in the trees framing her head. She is laughing. Delicate lines play at the edges of her eyes.

I am with Rabbia. She is pointing at the moon in the sky.
    She says, The ocean is moved by it. Why not you?
    I look up in wonder. I had not considered it before.
    She puts one hand on my womb and talks to me about water.
    I take a deep breath. I smell salt.

I am singing, and my voice rises to the top of the great white tent and slides out into the treetops covering the mountain. I am chanting, a prescription of names. As-Salam. The source of peace. Ash-Shahid. The witness. Al-Haqq. The truth. My beloved. If I say the names enough they will hold my center while I spin around the head of a nail, one hand raised, my eyes seeing beyond here, my ears peacefully holding onto the beat of the drum only.
    I am transcending. I spin and spin, my brothers and sisters tapping their fingers to the hyde of the daf to keep my heart tethered to the earth. They understand. I need this. I have seen them witness my eyes.
    They hold me in this space and time slips away.
    We are free here. We are one.

Rabbia sits across from me, our legs crossed. The soft hairs on the caps of our knees mingling. I feel such pleasure from this that I think of the ocean. I can hear the slow sound of a stream hiding in the woods. She cups her hands over my ears, little caverns to trap the sounds in my head.
    She says, Don't be afraid. What are they telling you?

I lay down on the nylon sleeping bag in my tent, no human sounds, the nearest human some miles off. I hear the bending of young trees, the rustling of brush. The tarp beneath me crinkles. I am alone and this is when strange things begin to happen. The silence makes me feel as though I am no longer contained. I want to cry for help. My voice is caught in my throat. As my mind decides to panic, my body chooses a great calm, an edge of sleep calm.

I listen. Really listen for the first time.

I laugh. I weep. Such immense sadness.

There is no thought attached to it. I open my mouth and I speak.

When everything is quiet again, I feel a knotty root has carved a home out of my hip, but there is no buzzing at my ears. I am at peace.

As-Salam. Ash-Shahid. Al-Haqq.

I step outside of my tent into moist earth, leveling prehistoric ferns with the soft soles of my feet. No, they have begun to form calluses by then. Just at the heels. The rocks beneath my feet hardly bother me.

The sun is setting, a blanket of pink tucking the mountain in to sleep.

We sit around the fire beneath the stars. Rabbia raises her daf to her cheek and sings into the skin, chains dangling from the frame scraping an eerie sound. She calls her ancestors, she calls the prophets. Rabbia's face distorted through the heat of the flames.

Rabbia tells me to think of the prophets. Maybe this is your path too.

She asks, Do you believe me?

I am tired. I am three years past the death of my mother, six years past the death of my first true teacher, and yet the flies keep circling my head. The only way to stop the hum is to speak it into the air, speak it plain.

I do not believe in that sort of thing. Abilities. Power stored in people, individuals who can speak for flies. Here in the mountains, there are so many things buzzing in the air. It is hard to tell sometimes what is my own. I hope that I am not speaking anything into existence.

I choose to answer a different question instead.

I tell her that she is pregnant.

In her eyes I see that it is possible.

I wonder if I ever had a chance.

Here is Rabbia, the space between her shoulder blades hugging the trunk of a tree. The fabric of her shirt is pulled up over her belly. It bulges, blue veins stretched beneath the skin. The color makes me think of flowers.

I am on my knees at her side. I put the pad of my forefinger on the button of her belly. I place the palm of my hand flat on her warm skin. She is watching me.

I fold over and kiss just above my thumb. I hold my lips there. I close my eyes. I lose myself for a moment. When I lift my head, there is a small diamond of moisture where my lips parted.

I look at Rabbia and her eyes say that she's sorry.

She places her hand over mine.

I can't stay here.

VIII.

I see the shore in front of me, I see a pink hair tie around my wrist, hard plastic bobbles intertwined, black bobby pins secured around it poke into the air like a sea urchin's spines. I am treading water. I raise one hand to scratch beneath the green sequined trim of my bathing suit. I feel my skin warm under my nails.

I am underwater and writhing.

I break through the surface. I gasp for air.

There is water all around me. I kick my feet, I try to feel for anything solid. My limbs aren't moving fast enough. They are heavy. My eyes are wide, stinging.

Warm air on my face, my hand. I am coughing. I am sputtering. My heart is racing, I can't breathe. I reach as far as I can into the air.

My mouth fills with water.

IX.

I tilt my head to see myself better in the window. This face of mine has become a moon too. My lower eyelids have widened, turned outward to face the world. Soft skin like pillows beneath them.

He squeezes his hand on her knee as we pull into another station. As he looks away, she makes eye contact with a man entering the train.

The man looks at me and his neck becomes rigid, then looks back at the couple. She tightens her grin. It is slow, deliberate. It's a rebuke. The man ignores her, walks to the other end of the car, away from me.

Her eyes drop to my lap. She cautions a glance up at me and then looks away, looks around. Her eyes land on an advertisement, stay there.

She was a quiet child. Her favorite game was hide-and-seek. The Christmas that she turned six, her cousins searched for two hours before she came out and surrendered. She was in the neighbor's dog house asleep.

I turn my head and let her hide.

X.

I see the moon pass over the head of a statue of a saint. I think of Rabbia. I wonder if it would be possible to find her after all of these years.

I watch a man pass on the sidewalk, and I sink back into the shadows of the abandoned church, stepping over an overgrown garden bed, backing into the wall. The bricks scratch at the skin sagging over my elbows. He does not see me.

I watch a cloud pass over the moon. I sit down to listen to the flies.

I stand in the park beside the river, waiting. I see her coming, walking along the path with her briefcase, the red glasses, the red hair. I call out to her. She stands still. She looks toward me. I am a stranger. I have frightened her. I hold up my hands, but I raise my voice so that she can hear me. I try to deliver the message quickly. I tell her to go back to daycare and check on her daughter. She's sick, a very high fever. She needs to go to the hospital.

What?

I say it once more. Her face contorts, and then her eyes wander as she thinks. She narrows her eyes at me before she turns back in the direction she came from.

I climb through the window at the back of the church. It has been left open for me. Inside, two of the women who have claimed this building are already asleep, curled up on their cardboard mattresses, each bundled in a heap of blankets.

I wake up to one pouring holy water over the crown of my head, the other swirling the fog of burning leaves over the length of my body. I am still. I let them work. Their hands hover above my body and whisper furiously.

When no demon flies from me to the mouse caged beside my head on the rotting wood floor, they declare that I am blessed. They ask me what I can tell them. I have nothing to say.

When the man who shares this space with us arrives, he is not convinced about the demon. The women watch as he ushers me over the padlocked fence.

I feel a burning in my knees as I land on the sidewalk. I bend over to massage them with my hands. I look up into the face of the statue budding between blades of overgrown grass. I believe it is St. John, the only apostle to die in old age, sound asleep.

XI.

I see the tire of my bicycle threading the yellow line in the center of the street. It is Saturday, listless. The hot sun beams overhead. I ride through the neighborhood to pick up Angie on my pegs. I tell her stories. I wander the aisles of the Stop & Shop peppered with sand, looking at little cakes so preserved they hold their shape when I drop them on the sidewalk later. I stand and watch the trains roll in from Manhattan. It's a new destination, the Rockaways. The city slickers pace the concrete while they squint in all directions.

Where? they ask.

This way? they squint.

Disoriented. Can't sense the water, can't see beyond a block. Too much sky, probably. They wander down my street and I point them in the right direction. I flick clods of dirt off of my porch while I wait for dinner.

XII.

I yawn.

Her eyes find me.

Do you want to look?

Her eyes drop to the speckled black tile of the train car. She plants a half smile on her face, knowing now that she is being watched. She is trying to look pleasant, innocuous.

Don't be afraid to look.

He clears his throat again and takes his phone out of his pocket. He busies himself with it.

You know, you understand. I see it in your eyes, but it isn't sad. Not a bad thing to be swept away. You understand the ocean? Yes? So endless. How could you know anything but up or down out there? Such powerlessness. Just a speck so small. You feel a sort of loss, you must, when you touch the world so closely.

Look at me.

She loosens her grip on his arm and looks up at me. Her eyes twitch as she tries not to look away. When they settle, it looks like she might cry. Her lips stretch into a flat line.

This is always happening, this coming and going away. There is no need to fear the ocean.

He looks up at me now too.

The tide moves in, moves out. It's always happening. Inevitable.

Natural light floods the train car, dazzling us with its presence. We are above ground. I look to the window and see the buildings passing through my face, the clouds. The rounds of my cheeks are settled low, creating a cavern around my mouth. I smile, my lips are thin, and the skin of my cheeks hardly moves. Nothing to fear there.

The train pulls into another station. They look through the window past my head. They both stand and adjust their coats.

The train doors open and a gust of cold wind washes over my face. That feeling like cold water. I nod at her. She nods back, smiles. They both exit the train.

I look out the window behind me, over the tracks, the ocean far out in the distance. Below, a small Black girl with her arms outstretched is working her way down the street, the front tire of her bicycle threading the yellow line.

XIII.

It is Sunday. I am stuffed in itchy shiny polyester, patent pinching Mary Janes, slick laminate pews, small ideas of heaven. It is a short walk down to the pier after the service. The women in their monochromatic skirt suits hold one hand to their hats.

I run down. The water is cold, eastern shores never warm for long. Bare ankles, the wash of the wave, coming and then going. Gooseflesh pushes the hairs out from their follicles. I rub my hand over the erect hair. The way that it scratches my palm.

Mother calls to me, Return. So many rumors about what is in the water. Purity. There is no purity left in the world, she says.

I look back at my mother. I see no fire, no brimstone. No need to rush.

Kelsey Monahan Stole Your Goddamn Jacket

You realize this after coming back from a visit with your umi. It will go the same way those visits always do. There's two kid siblings at home, and you're pretty sure your younger brother is queer too, so that's the only reason you bother going back. Umi will quietly ask if you want to visit the masjid down the street. Just to pray asr. You know asr will turn into whispered conversations with the imam which will turn into men reading Quran over you in the basement. The sheikh will scream surahs in your ear. They say if you flinch, you're possessed. Your mother will go upstairs, running tasbeeh through her hands, feeling groves you helped put there. Umi would rather have a daughter full of jinn than a daughter who fills herself with women.

The jacket will be the little thing that sets you off. It's a Goodwill jacket that most likely cost a dollar. Most likely, you didn't even buy it but slipped it on underneath the cascading fabric of your abaya. The workers in the suburbs haven't caught on to Muslim girls' tricks yet. Your brother broke an ink pen in the front pocket, so the ugly bloom is how you know it's yours when you see your roommate, Kelsey Monahan, sitting at the dinner table. In your fucking jacket.

Your caseworker has been helping you with managing your emotions. You'll see Kelsey Monahan at the table and make a quick roundabout back up to your room. You won't even say hello to the staff member in the kitchen, even though they're your favorite. The hallway on the second floor smells. It's cause people leave dirty tampons in the shower and throw the socks they masturbate with in the regular trash. You got a personal water bottle you use as a lota. You were not raised dirty.

Asia, your other roommate, will be on her bed when you come in. The two of you get along. The first time she came into the shelter, you read her name tag on the door before meeting her and ended up pronouncing her name the Muslim way, *Ah-see-a*. When you told her

Asiya is one of the four best women of all time, she said keep it. She liked it better than being named after a continent that wanted nothing to do with dark girls like her. You're the only one who gets away with saying her name like that.

She'll say something like, *Kels took your shit. You saw, huh?*

She won't have to look up from her phone. Y'all are good friends. She will read how anger sits in your steps.

You say, *You didn't stop her*, but raise the inflection so it's like a question. You are not beefing with Asia. You are beefing with Kelsey Monahan, who stole your fucking jacket.

Girl, she had that shit on when I came in. Asia will finally put her phone down. She might pat at her head, try to scratch between the braids cause the hair lady did them too tight again. You keep telling her to go to your friend over North, but she swears by the Ethiopian shops on the South Side. Never mind that her edges are running. She breaks out in blisters along her hairline every damn time. You figure, let her learn, and stop trying to say anything. She will look at you with one hand still on her head, ask, *Was it on your bed or something?*

It was in your hamper. You were about to wash it. That will make Asia snort, *That bitch went through your hamper.* She might even full out cackle, throwing herself back, quiet for a minute before she starts up again. *Those dirty bitches*, she'll lift her head to look at you, *I'd of got it back for you if I could, trust. But I'm on my second strike.*

Yeah, there are strikes where you are. Little things get you them. Talking back to staff, forgetting your daily chores, shit like that. When you get three strikes, the caseworkers kick you out for the night. It is probably not how things are supposed to go. The binder of guidelines they hand everyone to read on intake probably outlines a long, restorative process when someone reaches their three strikes. But things do not always work as written. You are all the best population to know this, so you do not bother to complain much.

Sure, most kids leave the house slamming doors, cussing. One time Alicia stood outside in the snow and pitched a fit so intense she ripped the screen door clean off. That got her another night out, but you all understood her rage. Most of you do not have someplace else to go. It's why you're here to begin with. Last time Asia got three strikes, you found her sleeping on the bench at the transit center downtown. Embarrassment made you both pretend to be strangers.

There are majors here too. Major violations. Fucking in the building, doing drugs, threatening staff, fighting. All of that gets you sent
out for good. Sometimes it happens right away. Sometimes you wait
until morning. You think that would be the worst. Having to lie in bed,
knowing tomorrow they will strip its sheets, wipe down the plastic
cover underneath, and pass it on to someone else. Meanwhile, you will
be standing on a corner with all your shit packed into garbage bags,
wondering what to keep, what to sell, and where to go.

You should not risk a major. They will call your mother because she
is still technically on your file. She will not call you, but she will call
your family. Tell all your cousins. You will see them downtown at the
Target that's easy to steal from, stuffing bags of chips under your winter coat, and know that they know all your damn business. But, more
than you cannot risk a major, you cannot risk being a punk bitch.

I'mma get my shit back, you will decide. You could sit on your bed
and wait to confront Kelsey Monahan later, when she eventually
comes back to sleep. You and Asia could throw her drawers on the
ground in the meantime, fake ignorance when she comes in like you
don't know who did it. But you are back from a visit with your umi,
who would rather send you into heavy basements of men than touch
you anymore. You brushed her hand on accident before asr, while taking a scarf from her hands, and she excused herself to remake wudu.
You are back from a visit with your umi and aware of how you carry
the wrong face. You thought coming back, maybe Musa will be fine.
Musa has your mother's nose, thin and pointed. Musa has your mother's small eyes, seeing only what they want to. Musa has your mother's
mouth, pursed at a world he hasn't known. If your mother knows Musa
craves boys the way you lay down for girls, he will weep, and she will
be able to see how she wounds herself. You are her distorted image.
You weep, and Umi calls it a haunting. You are back from a visit with
your umi and have a throat sore from whispering.

Asia will say, *Don't get yourself kicked out* and go back to her phone.
Or maybe she will say, *Don't.* Maybe, *That's not a good move.*

Maybe, *Sit down, chill with me.*

Or maybe you will simply whisper her decision, the last gentle de-
cree, and she will not hear it. Isn't that how you always do things?
Announcements in the middle of the night so no one else can testify.
Maybe you will not even speak. Maybe you'll slip out of the room. She

will only notice when the door clicks shut behind you.

Kelsey Monahan will be sitting downstairs at the dining table still, with her elbows on it because she has no respect. You will tie your hair into a bun as you come down the stairs. Your sneakers will be laced tight. She will look up at you when you come into the room. It is the smile on her face that will give you all the energy to walk right up next to her.

You're disrespectful as fuck, you'll say. *With your elbows on the table where people eat. With my damn jacket on.*

The only staff member is still in the kitchen, cleaning. You can hear the sounds of pots and pans crashing against each other as Kelsey looks up at you. She is not from here. She is from some town further north, where maybe she was the resident badass. Maybe she ran the streets there, but you cannot compare city pavement to country dirt roads. She has a background, a reason for being here that could be as complicated as yours, but you do not care.

Kelsey will respond. She will scoff or laugh or roll her eyes. For sure, she will say *nigga*. It will roll off her tongue, another stolen article she's been comfortable wearing for too long. She may say, *Nigga, you need to calm down.* Or, *It's not a big deal, nigga.* Or anything else to convey you are on equal ground. And she is down. And she is hip. And she is someone to be wary of, because nigga has soaked her tongue. You will latch onto that as your excuse. Tell her to get up. She will not. Tell her again, this time raising your voice. Maybe tack on a *bitch* at the end. Make it clear that you will swing on her sitting. That maybe it is in her best interest to stand. You will say, *I'm not your nigga,* and *That's not your jacket,* and you will leave unaddressed all the other things you want to reject being.

You will get the jacket back.

The sounds in the kitchen will stop as you both scream. The staff member will rush out to you holding Kelsey on the ground. Your mother taught you how to fight young. You sat on the kids in your masjid who used to tease you for wearing hijab wrong, as if you could control that afro hair makes a camel's bump. They will not be able to touch you. This is a facility that does not use physical restraint. Things do not always go by the book here, but that is one. The jacket will get tossed to the side. You will stand and kick at Kelsey's head.

Come with me, the staff member will say. *Grab your jacket.* And they will be sorry. In the nurse's office with the dim lighting, they will perch on a high stool and slump, *You know what the rules are. You signed to them when you came here. You agreed to no physical altercations.* Asia will watch from her bed as you pack. It will not be an official exit. You are supposed to come back in the morning to meet with your caseworker. *There may be something they can do*, the staff member will say, and you bite your tongue to say there is not.

Girl, Asia will sigh.

You'll shrug, *I got my shit back.*

It'll be the middle of winter. The buses do not run in the neighborhood except for once every hour. The staff member will shove a single token in your hand as if it will get you anywhere. There will be a frozen puddle on the sidewalk outside. You'll see your face in it thanks to the porch light. There will be a bruise blossoming under your left eye. The only good hit Kelsey Monahan got in. *Come back in the morning*, the staff member will say.

Do not call my mother, is all you'll say.

You will walk. Your phone will ring in your pocket, and if you pull it out, you will see your mother's face fill the screen. If you answer, you will hold the phone to your ear and make sure your teeth do not chatter in the cold. Your mother's voice will sound full of sleep. *I had a dream about you.*

You will pause where you are. Shrug on the jacket, pull the collar up to protect your neck. You'll pull your scarf down on your forehead and tighten it, as if your mother can see. You will flex the fingers of a hand already turning numb. Your mother taught you to recognize dreams as intuition. To give them weight and recognition. It is dreams that started the chain effect to bring you here in the first place. Your mother will clear her throat, repeat, *I had a dream. About you.* And you'll say, *Subhanallah.*

Umi, tell me about it.

The Goodbye Sister

I loved visiting my younger sister when she lived at the modern brickwork complex around Shell Gas Station. You had to pull the bell of the northbound Route Sixteen bus right at that exact moment and cross the dangerous curved street with no stoplights, watching for incoming traffic aiming in both directions.

We had many girl's nights there. Just us and Donatos thin crust pizza with all the vegetable toppings and those amazing cinnamon-sugar dough balls for dessert. Sometimes, if we had a real good coupon deal, breadsticks would be in the order too.

She selected eclectic film combinations from the library. For instance, Gene Hackman and Denzel Washington battled wills in *Crimson Tide*, and afterward we read subtitles of French animated *Triplets of Belleville*. Our penchant for Brian White films included the soft comedy *Mr. 3000*, dark erotic *Trois*, and Black spiritual romance *Me and Mrs. Jones*.

Then I would crash on her soft beige wrap around couch, warmed by her extra blankets, full of love and food. The large windows were closed by long white blinds that touched wall-to-wall carpeting, a deep, pretty gray.

Her belongings were neatly arranged; different from the chaotic dolls, clothes, and coloring books splattered on our shared childhood bedroom floor.

She resided in one of the best places ever acquired by any of us.

I sat on the rickety bus quietly, having returned back to small-town Ohio life, stirred by never-ending fantasies that my sister would return to the cusp of a family consumed by her painful absence. We loved her dearly. Love wasn't enough for someone who wanted to break free from the cycle of miserable oppression festering in our genes like an incurable disease.

"Why do you always go back?" she asked constantly.

I looked out the bus window and observed an endless line of dilapi-dated houses, unfinished projects, and charred arsonist efforts that documented an economically salvaged town. In turn, vulnerable gate-ways accepted the gnawing pity and despair. This parasitic village stole souls of those wallowing and wasting away in the awful, disturbing quicksand, preventing the mentally shackled feet from fleeing an oth-erwise sunken place.

"If I could leave, I would never come back," she vowed passionate-ly. "There is nothing to come back to."

Not even family could trap her independence.

At times, I envied her stout commitment. She stayed true to herself, to her obstinate beliefs. Often, I longed to disappear entirely without leaving behind any visible traces. It simply wasn't possible. These peo-ple were like magnets. Whenever a resemblance akin to hatred entered my reactionary thoughts, it was temporary. Months would pass. I couldn't resist seeing the family due to morbid responsibility, a stern misguided desire for acceptance in the arms of toxicity. They could be so cruel, so selfish. And she had known it.

One year, she gifted me gorgeous glow-in-the-dark celestial curtains. I packed them from one place to the next. They didn't glow anymore. Yet her spirit was ever active in these fourteen-year-old objects, a sheer universe of white stars, moons, and suns filling a dark blue void. She bought them because they matched my blanket and pillow set.

I only kept her curtains.

As the bus neared the gas station, I pulled the yellow cord.

The complex still looked the same, impressive and brown, the black iron-like stable legs keeping it together. My sister stayed in the second building, the steps to her door on the far right end.

I crossed the street and searched around, hoping her essence lin-gered in this direction, lost and asking for guidance. I could envision her laughing and eating pizza. The tomato sauce would make a subtle mess of her face, and she would swipe it off with complimentary white napkins.

"I am back," she said, affectionately cupping my cheeks with her lengthy, delicate fingers. It was like nine years hadn't idly passed by, that the yesterday was just a yesterday, and not two leap years, four hundred sixty-eight weeks, and three thousand two hundred eighty-seven days and counting.

"It's good to see you," I said, not minding that her hands were practically icicles.

She would go above and beyond a younger sister's duty, bringing out an utterly whole and beautiful validity in ways our guarded mother or unaffectionate brothers weren't capable of expressing.

"Where have you been?" I asked.

"Around," she replied cryptically, still smiling, her thin raisin lips framing perfect white teeth.

Why were we meeting here? She hadn't lived in this apartment for almost ten years.

First, she lived in Cincinnati, then up to Chicago, moved to somewhere in Minnesota, and dissolved in San Francisco, immersed into a million people, a million possibilities, only to be lost forever.

We were last together during a summery Denver, playing Scrabble with lush cats while a Stephen King VHS tape clicked in the background. She had come to visit me straight out of Minnesota, traveling with church people that she recently met. She was an outgoing, affable personality, making friends everywhere. I inherited our mother's awkward introversion, preferring isolation over the vexing company of others.

My sister, however, would be my constant exception.

During our week together, I introduced her to Tegan and Sara, Nneka. She outplayed the heck out of them. We bonded over this new girl named Janelle Monae, and she excitedly said that they locked eyes at her concert. She tried to teach me to ride the bike after it rained, holding the handlebars with me. When she let go, I screamed like a frightened child, foreseeing unhealable scars in the future.

On the second to last day, we had a huge fight. During the passive silence, she took off with the bike, going on solitary adventures, likely turning more strangers into temporary friends.

The morning of her plane ride to California, our hug was stiff and frigid. She left behind a beautiful Mahogany Hallmark card of three Black girl angels that opened up in three. Inside, she wished me Happy

Birthday a month and a half early.

An incredible sadness ignited that day, an unhealed sadness because that was our physical departure.

We called and texted. Yet the trip had damaged us. Some stupid, insignificant grudge that I allowed to manifest with my icy silence.

I won't be communicating for a while, she texted out of the blue in late November.

How long is a while? I asked.

Just a while.

One by one, she deleted her social media pages. I emailed her some months later and it ricocheted back.

"This user no longer exists."

Her final text message had been a Bible quote from either Psalms or Revelation or Proverbs. I saved it long after her number had been disconnected. The tone was definitely "goodbye."

I spent days rereading old emails. Between dead birthday eCards and short hellos, she sent film suggestions (most I had seen) enclosed with her passwords on inactive film sites, a piece with evidence to stay away from soy, and a beginning of a gritty unfinished short story.

Time progressed and separation was agonizing torment. A fiercely important part had been ripped out of my body and I could not function properly without it.

In dreams, she would be this untouchable entity that felt simultaneously authentic and false.

She had the mannerisms, yes, but she was jarringly different to an almost frightening degree. She did have hot streaks of aggressiveness that could dagger a heart, but her goodness broke through generational inclination to inflict such blistering verbal violence.

The latest dream was last night.

We were riding in our uncle's car - my mother's handsome older brother - and heading toward the family, extremely happy to be together after so much time apart.

"We're going home," our uncle said, his hands tightly gripping the steering wheel, looking back and forth between us with awe.

Our mother despised her family and hadn't spoken to them in years. That wasn't on my mind with my alive sister in the backseat.

"We're going home," she repeated.

I saw her face in the rearview mirror. She hadn't aged a day - still twenty-four and not quite embracing the reality of turning thirty-three.

"We're going home," I said, sweetly comforted by the familiar euphoria that had been desperately missing.

For an hour, I sat on the nearby park bench, imagining that she had been hiding in plain sight all along, in that great big apartment eating Donatos and watching occasionally skipping library films.

That sharp intuition told her to pause everything. The second floor door burst open and she stood out like a radiant present to the world that mourned her absence. She looked down and saw a sister patiently waiting.

"Welcome back," she would greet me, smiling with tomato sauce on her stubborn chin.

In c/o Chidi Onyeachu

They only do this in Black neighborhoods, keep people waiting all damn day. When the Post Office closes at five and doesn't open until nine, don't they know people have jobs? Tamika taps her tan mules. She's seventh or eighth in line, after waiting fifteen minutes already. She hates knowing, just as well as anyone else, that this is to be expected at Harlem's College Station.

Tamika looks behind her, finding a woman with a big box hitched to her hip like a toddler. She raises her eyebrows, projecting *Now isn't this some shit.* The woman shakes her head, and Tamika watches the way her black bob moves, stiff with product. Her kaleidoscopic leggings with a small hole in the thigh and fuzzy purple slide-ons, the kind Rihanna made popular, make her errand look erratic, nothing like Tamika's own.

The box Tamika is carrying isn't too big, but it's heavy, and something seems to be reaching out of it, clawing at her forearm. Her waist too. *If I could just get this shit over with.*

She moves the package as far away from her body as possible.

Tamika has settled well into her pretty. The hair she stopped straightening when it broke off in college is mounted into a high pineapple. Her brown polka-dotted dress, with spaghetti straps and sleeves that hang off the shoulder, hits mid-thigh, and the additional height of her two-inch mules makes her look like a model. Her face is plain, but also scar and pimple-free; a rich brown that is hard to classify. She is the type of woman whose physical attributes and staggering confidence bounce off each other, making others unsure of which came first.

"Excuse me, ma'am?" Tamika calls to the front of the line. The woman is older, short with age, her thin grey hair tucked under a solid blue baseball cap. Her right hand holds onto a cart, and her left clutches a pink package slip. "How long have you been waiting?"

The woman gives a pitying smile. "Since 8:55."

Shit. There's no way I'm getting all the way to Soho by ten. "I'm going to be late for work again," Tamika says to no one in particular, but everyone in front of her seems to hold their breath. The line becomes stiller than it was before, and she knows without asking that nobody on this here sanctified Monday morning is giving up their spot.

She looks behind her again, this time past the kaleidoscopic leggings to a white woman, the sole white woman in line, her chin tilted toward the speckled ceiling as if perseverance would create the privilege she's used to. Tamika reminds herself that today is supposed to be a good day, an empowering day. She turns forward, grips her 10x10-inch package tight, waiting, not minding the sensation of a thousand needles prickling her hands.

She met Chidi at a Running Collective that held a standing 5K out of Marcus Garvey Park every Tuesday. Her stride was long, her spandex shorts gripped her thighs like a doctor's sphygmomanometer, and she could hear Chidi's quick, measured gasps behind her. Always right behind her.

She ran faster, if for no other reason than to get him off her back. She didn't mean to be judgmental, but he was an awfully big boy to be keeping up with the eight-minute milers. Thick from the neck down in a way she knew she wouldn't mind intimately, but thought confounding under the late afternoon sun. Shoulders with a wingspan twice her own, and a middle that she'd barely be able to wrap her arms around. And tall too; at least 6'3" or 6'4". He was what her girlfriends called "tied to the ground."

It was like having King Kong on her heels. And with the Collective's ban on headphones, she couldn't drown him out, not even with the children's song that played in her mind on repeat. *The ants go marching down, to the ground, to get out of the rain, boom, boom, boom, boom...*

It took Chidi four weeks to say anything to her, and when he did, all he said was, "You're fast." Bracing his hips in a way she could tell he was aching to sit down, panting, a smile across his face.

"No, I'm just faster than you," she said, hands clasped on top of her head. She was cooler than him, and it felt good to be cooler and faster.

He laughed loud. "Touché. But maybe I like running behind you?"

This nigga, she thought. *Basic.* "That's creepy, not cute," she said, withdrawing from the conversation, beginning to walk past him.

He reached for her arm but stopped short, brought his hand back quickly, knowing the decision wasn't a good one, and he was right.

She stared at her forearm where he'd almost touched her, eyes boiling. "I'm not a piece of chicken, you know. You can't just grab me."

It's always the cute ones who don't hold their hands accountable, the cute ones who reach and reach until they have you in a place that you haven't agreed to.

This one wasn't cute enough to risk the chance.

By the time Tamika reaches the front of the line, she has resigned herself to the wait, so the scowl on the clerk's honeycomb-colored face doesn't break her own bright red smile. "I just need to send this to -"

"Yep, just write the address there."

"Great. Do you have a pen?"

The clerk is blank-faced for a long time before slowly shaking her head. Raising her eyebrows, simultaneously answering and condemning the question.

Tamika rolls her eyes, looks behind her to the line that has grown with time. Next to the white woman, a lady wearing a tight red dress and matching red Converse stands out. Tamika makes eye contact with her.

"Does anyone in here have a pen?"

It is not the lady in the red dress or the white woman who comes up with a pen, but a little girl holding her mother's hand. She rummages through her backpack and pulls out a royal blue ballpoint. Her mother does not realize she is running to give it to Tamika until their grasp is broken.

"Ma'am. Ma'am!"

Tamika turns around.

It's the clerk.

"Please step aside while you take care of that. There's a line."

The nerve. Tamika moves to the side anyway. She tries to place the package on the sliver of counter that leads to the bulletproof glass, but cannot let it go. She resorts to writing with her non-dominant hand, uncapping the pen with her mouth.

Now the package has cut so deep into her right hand that it is bleeding, and her left hand is shaking with fear. She's holding the pen so tightly that her fingers are turning white, and she almost stabs a hole in the slip. She tries not to think about it, but sees Chidi's smile in the back of her mind; wide, glaring, an expressway of big teeth gated by even bigger lips. She cannot tell if his smile is genuine or mischievous.

In between the two windows, Tamika may as well have had the devil on one shoulder and an angel on the other.

To her right, a second clerk's bubbly chatter proves she hasn't worked there for long; with an untainted attitude like that, she couldn't have. "Next," she calls, much louder than the other clerk, who only mumbles it reluctantly.

As Tamika writes in generously loopy cursive, she can hear the white woman's flip-flops smack across the vinyl tiles, and then her relaxed white woman voice as she addresses the second clerk, "Did you have an all right weekend?"

It's just like some white woman to try to show everyone else up, giving out her niceness like a party favor, in exchange for what? Of course, she doesn't have as many reasons to be fed up, hasn't even registered what the ratchetness of this post office says about the neighborhood.

Tamika resents how nice her package looks, taped to perfection.

Bet it's not stabbing the life out of her. Bet she hasn't ripped it apart and put it back together a million times.

The second clerk answers the white woman pleasantly.

"Not so bad. Yours?"

"It was okay, thank you for asking."

In a whirl, the white woman is done, and Tamika hears the loud smack of her flip-flops again as she heads out the door.

He told her his full name on their second date. Zikoranachidi Onyeachu. And it was a seal, a name she could hold onto. And how well she remembered her own name in his mouth.

She liked it best when he imitated the way his father said it when they met for the first time - a flat, dramatic emphasis on *Tami*, the *ka* an afterthought, so it sounded more like *Tommyka*.

That Chidi's practiced replica could almost change her name entirely employed her, and whenever Chidi told her something he thought she should already know, this was the playful way he said her name.

"Ah, Tommyka, Tommyka o," he'd say, "I tell you this before."

And she felt solid and present and tied to the ground.

On the other hand, he shortened her name when they lay in bed, comfortable. "Mika, Mika, Mika," he'd say, scratching her scalp, making sure not to pull his fingers through her curls, but planting them firmly and moving his clipped nails less than a centimeter back and forth. It was an intimacy she needed more than she wanted.

"What am I going to do with you?" he'd ask, and she wondered if he was talking about her or the kinks that held his fingers captive. Either way, she felt another version of herself, lighter, wing bearing.

She didn't mean to fall in love with a man who could change her being with just the deportation of a syllable or the pronunciation of a vowel. It just happened.

Two people later, Tamika is back in front of the disgruntled clerk. This time, she takes a second to register her face, the brows that have almost grown together shading eyes dark enough to be mirrors.

Before she can get a word out, the clerk holds up a finger that she doesn't lower before taking an exaggerated breath. "Are you ready?"

"Well, I wanted to ask you...I don't know the apartment number. I mean, I can't remember it, but do you think it will still make it to my boyfriend?" *My boyfriend. A lie.*

The clerk lifts an eyebrow. "Without the complete address?"

"Well, it's most of the address."

"But it's not the complete address?"

"Technically?"

"There's only one definition for complete."

Tamika looks up, her eyes starting to water.

Dammit. I said I wouldn't cry.

"Okay, well, then I don't really know what to do." Her voice shakes. "This has to go out. I mean, I've been waiting a long time to send it. It's supposed to go out today, finally. It has to go out today. I'm thirty-five years old. I turned thirty-five last week, you know."

For the first time all morning, the clerk softens.

"Can't you call? Get the complete address?"

Tamika shakes her head. Chidi was very clear with his request that she send it if they were to speak again. That he receive it first, feel it in his hands, proof that her words weren't liquid, that they wouldn't slip between his fingers and drip from his knuckles like fufu dipped in

"And it can't wait? What are you sending him?"

Tamika rolls her eyes. *Nosy ass clerk. It's obvious how she will respond if I tell her, and sure, I shouldn't give a shit, but I do.* "It's...um..."

"What?"

"I don't know if..."

"If what?"

"Maybe I'll just..."

"Just what? Are you bleeding? You might want to do something about that hand."

Damn, can I get a word in?

"I don't think we have any Band-Aids here. I'm not even sure I should be handling your package when..." the clerk speaks absentmindedly.

She's had it. Tamika feels like she's going to scream. Maybe she does, in fact, scream.

"Dammit. It's my heart! I'm sending him my heart. Are you happy now?"

She must be screaming, because there's a collective gasp from the line. They've all heard, each and every brown face behind her. A wave of silence rings loudly, an aftershock. Even the package is quiet now, no longer stabbing her.

Tamika turns around and sees the mother first, her hands over her daughter's ears, her face creased with concern. Tamika knows what she must be thinking - it's been a long time since a woman has sent her heart through the mail. It's practically unheard of these days.

Finally, a voice from the audience, a woman wearing a Howard baseball cap and mom jeans, a starched New York accent.

"Girl, *what?*"

The last time something like this happened, something like this wasn't loud. Back then, a woman could send her heart and no one would be around to say anything about it. Women squeezed their whole bodies into boxes, pretzeled worse than Auntie Anne's. No one said a damned thing if a woman folded herself like origami into a loosely taped package and mailed her ass halfway across the world.

They were living together when Chidi said, "Come with me to LA."

It was a year and change into what he called the only healthy relationship he'd ever had. He wasn't shy about saying that he'd cheated on past girlfriends and hadn't been spared the karma. He wasn't shy about anything really, not even things Tamika thought he would be shy about; his ADHD, his salary, his aversion to love. He didn't use the word "love" romantically.

"Don't get all into grips when I don't say it," he said.

When he reiterated, "Come to LA, I'll take care of you," he was spread out on the couch, kicked back in sweatpants with a hoodie over his head. Even though Chidi paid $1800 a month, he didn't control the heat, and it was cold in there.

His casualness confused her.

"What do you mean?"

"I got the job!" His smile engulfed her, and she giggled without thinking.

Slowly processing, she said, "I thought you were applying just to see if you could. You said you didn't really want to move to the West Coast."

"That was before I got it."

She rolled her eyes.

"So you just up and leave me? Like that?"

"No." He sat up, making room on the couch for her. He tapped the open seat and she took it tentatively, "You can come with me. You hate your job, anyway. You can spend some time designing. That's what you've been wanting to do. This is going to be a win-win. I'll take care of you."

He's just like the rest of them, always thinking a woman wants a man to take care of her. Well, this woman doesn't.

"You want me to follow you across the country, be tied and dependent on you, give you a reason to act any old way and make me feel like I can't leave you?"

"I would never do that. Treat you any old way? You know better."

"I don't. Time takes its toll on relationships."

"But I'm making a commitment. What if I make a real commitment?"

She wondered if he was implying what she thought he was implying. Knowing neither of them was ready.

She wanted the proposal more than anything she could imagine;

something she could hold onto, rotating metal around her ring finger.

"What do you mean?" she asked.

"You know what I mean."

"Then go ahead, ask me."

He sighed, pulled his hoodie off, grabbed her shaking hand.

He stared at it for a long time.

"I don't think we should rush things just because..."

Asshole. She pulled her hand back. "You're smoke. I see right through you." She stood up and crossed her arms.

"I..." he paused, still unable to say it. Love was a word. It shouldn't have been all that he was making it. "You know how I feel."

"How?"

"*How?!*"

Silence. No one ever blamed it for its misgivings. Chidi was there to blame instead. *Fuck this wordless nigga.*

"I'll help you pack," Tamika said, "but after that, you're on your own."

Truth is, she didn't learn the truth until months, almost a year later. Tamika realized she wanted to be overwhelmed with Chidi. It was better than being overwhelmed with the ways of the world.

When one of her white colleagues said, "You can't be mad at everything," she thought of Chidi forgetting to put the cap back on the toothpaste. And when the death of Nia Wilson crossed her Twitter feed, she thought of Chidi placing his order at restaurants before she had enough time to make up her mind. And when one of her Black brothers said an award-winning Black female comedian needed to prove herself first, Tamika thought of Chidi using the microwave and touching the salt shaker and opening the refrigerator door with greasy fingers.

It hit her when a man on the street carrying cowrie shells asked, "Why are you so mad?"

She hated when men asked questions like that, like they cared, like their words were anything but an insult. Even more, she hated the way she always answered and argued with them in her mind. She couldn't ignore their insistence that her smile was more important than whatever she was frowning about.

She wondered, was she mad at Trump's immigration policies? Or was she mad because she wasn't with Chidi? Who better to have her heart than a man with a last name like Onyeachu. Than a man who'd started to run five miles every morning so he could keep up with her.

Than a man who danced with his knees, singing, *if I tell you say I love you, o.*

When a man let love burst through his pores like sweat, what did round words matter?

Now, the lights in the post office brighten and focus off-center. Tamika is cast in a half shadow.

"Oh sweetie, you can't send that," says the mother.

"Why not?" Tamika asks, turning to the line.

"It'll kill you, sis," says the Howard baseball cap.

"It's not something you can really part with, you know," argues the red dress with red Converse.

"Bet," the Howard baseball cap says.

"Well, what if she…" An older woman turns to address Tamika instead of the crowd. "What if you send him just part of it instead? Half of it?"

"Too risky." The red dress.

"You're trippin'." The Howard baseball cap.

"Almost doesn't count." The mother.

Tamika thinks they're only saying this because they haven't been in love. They haven't danced with a Nigerian man who flies just above the seventh octave.

"Even if I send it Priority? Insured? Express?" Tamika asks over her shoulder, to the second clerk, hoping to receive the pleasantries that were so gracefully offered the white woman.

"Go ahead, baby. Allow yourself to be soft." A new woman in the line takes a stand. She is wearing a satin dress. It's teal and falls from her shoulders seductively. She looks young, but her confidence points to just short of middle age.

"Soft? Do you fucking hear yourself?" The Howard baseball cap's voice rises. It is aggressive and pointed, and her moving hands work hard to match it.

"What? A Black woman has to be hard all the time? Glass is hard, and you can break it easier than anything." The woman in satin does not engage the Howard baseball cap's urgency. Her voice is languid.

"She ain't lied. Don't let anybody dictate what you do with your pussy." The red dress has a change of heart.

But now the room is agitated with mumbles because it hadn't been about that. This was bigger than sex.

"Y'all, please stop giving this woman advice. She's just going to do whatever she wants to do." The Howard baseball cap.

The room goes silent, save their lewd, loud eyes, imploring and demanding, all on Tamika. She comes from a two-story home just outside of Detroit. Her parents are still together, a mechanical engineer and an assistant professor. She has two younger sisters in their twenties, both doing well for themselves. She's never lost anyone, never known anyone close to her to abuse drugs or alcohol. Her life has never been hard outside of the everyday offenses issued a loud Black woman from The D. Some might say there is no excuse for Tamika's behavior, even if Chidi's life hasn't been as easy.

"Well," the silence is broken, a toad's croak. Tamika turns and spots the clerk's tire in the form of a nearly imperceptible wrinkle that starts in her eyebrows and ends at the point of her chin. "Put a fucking stamp on it," she says.

But Tamika can't move. And it seems as if the package itself has gone to sleep.

Maybe tomorrow, she thinks. Maybe she'll wait until tomorrow. Maybe tomorrow it will be easier to relinquish her heart than to listen to it.

Sitting Spells

When I open the door she just trots in, all prancing and sweet, high stepping like she helping the earth to turn, I tell you. I know by the way she sits down, selecting a chair to sit in before she is invited to rest her feet, that she was a child with little enough of *no* and too much of *anything you want baby*. But tell you the truth, I also recognize an old charcoal drawing of myself in her carriage, so I just laugh.

"What brings you here?" I ask as if I don't know. Pretty girl like her, nice clothes, new bag, polished nails, flower perfume, ain't but one thing she want: love. And with her, I can tell it isn't love in general, but one particular man she wants.

I know too, it was my sister who sent her up here. My sister got a glowing stripe of cruel running thick across her forehead. Had it tattooed there so everybody would be warned. Most folks can't see it though. Me, I lived with it most of my sixty-two years.

"Your sister Meecha told me to come and bring you this fruit and these flowers cut from her garden." She has a little hummingbird buzz of a voice.

"Hrmmph," I answer, but she doesn't notice.

I planted the damn flowers. Planted them when Meecha was sick and was just vomiting up all the spells I had talked her into making for me.

She warned me about the meaning of forever, but to a young girl in love, forever has about the same amount of sense as dandelion blossoms made outta concrete. It's just not something you want to consider. And always, well always is the wind young people dance on, so what was I to know. Yeah, I cried so long and hard, stopped sleeping, mostly stopped eating until she promised she would do what she could do to give me what I wished for. But she warned me there would be a price.

She made me learn how to brew some simple healing teas, which I mixed for her until she was well. Then I went and picked the other plants like she told me; some at the darkest part at night pulling them up from the roots, others just as dawn broke, breaking off only the smallest of leaves, and a few with their flowers in full bloom and full of nectar cut from underneath a perching bee while the sun was high and burning up the sky.

Always before I cut or pulled or plucked, I had to ask permission, like the plant gonna yell out, *No!* But I know even though plants can't stop me picking them, they can sure enough stop me from getting to their power. So I did it all, paying attention to the slightest detail because I wanted what I wanted, and I'd do what I needed to do to get it.

Well finally, after weeks of preparing the herbs, she fed the brew to me. At first swallow, it was almost sticky sweet, but as I took in each sip, it became more and more bitter. But I kept on till every drop was gone.

As soon as I drank it down, she took out her bone-handled blade, cut a small nick right above my heart and swallowed three drops of blood. Before I knew it, Meecha was vomiting and coughing and then retching up some more. It turned from yellow and orange to green and finally was laced with a little blood. I caught the blood and dug it into the dirt around the Bird of Paradise I had planted for her the year before. Those birds just opened up their orange feathers and arched their green backs and sucked it up. Meecha got well, and my problem was as good as it was gonna get solved until he ate the special stew.

Meecha promised me that the stew was gonna fix it up forever. Meecha said it could only happen once and I had to choose the meal. Said it would be my last, very last chance to change my mind.

My sister warned me that if I went all the way, there was a price, a heavy price. She said it from the day before I used the spell and she repeated it every year from then until now when I would start to whine. And every time some young girl asked her for the spell of forever love, she would make them wait. She would make them wait until the Bird of Paradise bloomed.

Then when the flowers opened their purple beaks, if the girl was still mooning around Meecha's front porch, Meecha would cut down two blooms and have some or another child bring them up to me so I could testify to how well her spells worked.

"Meecha said I should ask you." That's what the girl is saying, halfway pleading and halfway demanding. I just stand there waiting for her to finish. "She said I should ask you how well her spells work. Ask you what you think about forever love."

I don't say nothing, just look at her. This one, she got the shiniest brown eyes I've seen in a long time, all full and round and bulging out of their sockets, wanting to see everything. And when she talks it's like she's laughing at the same time. Seem like she wouldn't need nothing to help her along. But then that's what Meecha told me about myself. This child's head is probably just as hard as mine.

She opens her pretty leather satchel and pulls out a small package wrapped in red cellophane and a white kerchief. "Also, I brought this lace handkerchief and a small rum cake. I baked it myself."

That's good, I think. *Has some sense anyway.* Coming visiting and wanting something from a neighbor who is a half step away from being a stranger. Coming with nothing but an *I need* and *you should give me*. I don't think so. Not in this house.

Well she is smiling at me and I see she got a little mischief behind those eyes. Just a foolish girl I tell you, foolish, but bright at the same time. Maybe, maybe this one will hear me.

"I brought the bottle with the rest of the rum too."

And the girl opens up her satchel again, pulls out some Appleton's and we both start to rolling. Meecha doesn't approve of spirits. She says they muddy the waters. I say sometimes you got to muddy the water to find a gold nugget. So I make us up some tea and fill the cups with honey and then pour a shot of rum into each one. I slice the rum cake real thin and see it's all dark and moist and full of fat amber and purple apricots and currents, and a smile breaks out in spite of myself.

"Child what you need with Meecha? You doin' fine."

"I love him so much I can't breathe sometimes."

She says it just like that. Her mouth so fulla her fantasy she can't even hold all that syrup inside.

"It's not just his look, although he does make my eyes get bigger to fit alla him in. And it's not just his smell, although he smells like moss and cinnamon. And his voice mmm, deep like the rumble of thunder way off in back of the mountain. And his touch..."

At that, she sees I am staring at her like she is stark raving mad.

"And he's smart too and has a job, and he'll fight if he has to but wouldn't never lay a violent hand on me," she says, finishing her list with a flourish, as if to let me know she's not so foolish as to want a do nothing, no good man.

"He sounds just about perfect."

"And perfect for me too, in every way. You should see how we look good together. He even says how good we look walking down the street together, or making love, or well, we just look good together like a matched set."

"Well then what you need with Meecha?"

"He's not the staying type."

"So then you need to figure he's yours to have and not to keep. Like this rum. When you finish it up, you get another bottle."

"Folks say he could be mine to keep. They say Meecha, she has the power."

"Well my name isn't Meecha, it's Rhea," I say, knowing perfectly well that that is not what I'm supposed to say. That it won't be enough. That Meecha will make my life even more miserable if I don't let this girl know about the choice she's making. Because Meecha, see, she does what she is asked. You pay her the money and if she can get that Geechee going - well you have your wish. Some kinda way you have it. Meecha is an honest woman. Cold witch of a sister, but honest. Cruel but honest.

The girl just sits there and then starts laughing and reaches out her hand to shake mine.

"Unetha. I'm sorry to be so rude. My name is Unetha Jackson and I am pleased to formally meet you, Rhea. I've seen you before at the market and once with your sister at the street festival."

We so past that I don't know what to say. Just then I see Herman walking down the road toward my front door. He's two steps closer than he was the last time. I go pull shut my curtains and then he turns around and walks away. I know I have a thin line of sweat covering my top lip. I hope Unetha doesn't see it.

"Honey if that man he makes you feel all fine and tingly, and that's all he has to give, you need to take it and be happy. Or else let it go and find another one. That's the truth of it."

"I don't want another one, I want him. Meecha said that I had to talk with you before she would give me the potion that will do the job."

"Potion is just to give you something to do. She does all the first work child, and then you do all the work after that."

I can't help myself. I start laughing, pick up the cup, and empty it. Then I motion to her, "Drink up baby, drink up. You think we old women forgot what it is to be in love? Think we don't need to feel the sweet sap curling our gardens, don't have any bend and stretch to wrap our full wrinkled limbs around honey? I tell you girl, some of us have stopped, but me - I'm still plenty alive. And I remember being so full of someone I didn't hardly have room for food, and you can see..."

I pat my full hips and run my hands down my thick, shiny forearms. "I'm not one to miss too many meals. Like my men like I like my meals. Full of spice and color."

I'm laughing and making myself another toddy. "I'm going to tell you everything Meecha wants you to know. And maybe something that she don't. So drink up. Drink up."

She takes another swallow and then takes off her shoes. I smile as she curls her legs up under her butt and refills her cup.

"I was about your age, how old are you baby, twenty-three, twenty-four?"

"Twenty-four last Thursday, that's why I need to get this one and settle down."

"Hrmmph." I bite my tongue. Got her three more lifetimes in front and trying to force one door shut while kicking down another. More than splinters gonna be filling up her arms and legs. More than splinters.

"Well I was twenty-two and this man I just had to have, hmm, well he was red-brown like a ripe pecan and seemed like he was so tall I had to lean my head back to see all of him. And child when he laughed, I felt like someone had just pulled a piece of silk slow across my body softly stroking me from my toes up through the crown of my head. And he had one gold tooth in his mouth that sparkled whenever he laughed. Child he could take all your salt and turn it to a cup full of sugar with one of his smiles. And he was a hard worker too, like your honey. What you say his name was baby?"

"I didn't say."

"Doesn't make me no never-mind, child. None at all. Well my honey, first time he leaned into me I wanted to run with the heat that rose up between us, it was so thick I could almost hold onto it. He put his finger under my chin, lifted up my face and barely brushed my lips with his. I thought he'd do more but he just barely touched them, and I was ready to just fall all over him, but he backed off saying, *You so sweet Rhea, if I take too much I swear I'll lose all my teeth to cavities.*

"We had met up at the flea market. I was helping Meecha sell her soaps and lotions and candles. We always did quite well. That was before we got the store. Everyone wanted Meecha's oils, still do. Well this day I had gotten hungry and walked off to get Meecha and me some grilled corn. I always went to his stand, his and his Uncle's. He always would give me the corn for free and blink his big eyes at me and then cast them down like he was shy. Always claimed to be shy, said he had to look down 'cause I was so pretty and shined so bright I just made it impossible for him to see anything else. Child, he was such a beautiful liar.

"This particular day when I got there, he asked me to take a walk with him. Said he knew where to get the best ginger beer to go with the corn. Well I was thirsty, and I had been hoping to talk to him without his uncle or my sister being a part of the conversation, so I walked with him. Before I knew it, we were at the edge of the market and behind a stand selling tall armoires and dressers. Well he just stopped walking all of a sudden, faced me and just looked at me. Child, I stopped breathing. My chest started hurting and I felt my cheeks burning, and then he bent over and just brushed my lips and then backed off. I wanted more but didn't get any, not that day. But the next week I went to his stall again and this time before I reached the row where it was set, he met me and took my hand, and we just walked around the market looking at Maggie's purses and Jerome's hand-knit hats, and he bought me a little carved hummingbird from old Keho."

"That old man was carving then too? I have one of his birds."

"Course you do child, course you do."

I smile. How amazing that all that naive could fit around all that stubborn. I can see her as clear as fresh river water, clear as the cloudless sky.

"The beak was so sharp it actually pricked me. I was startled, and my love, he just smiled and took my hand to his mouth and kissed it so soft right where the carved beak had pierced. And then as he moved to my lips I turned my head away, and he caught the nape of my neck and kissed it, and I felt a shiver swell up and just make my insides start jiggling like a bowl of Jell-O. He put his hand around my waist, and we walked outside the market toward the parking lot. Then he leaned me up against one of the trucks and bent me back and filled my mouth with his tongue, slow and searching like he wanted to know me, really know me not just get up in me. He stroked his hands up my thighs and just when I don't know if I'm going to pull my legs apart or clamp them shut he pull back and tells me that my sister is probably starting to miss me, and we should get back. We quick set up a time to meet later that evening."

I'm looking at Unetha. She is only half listening to me. I see her remembering her first kiss with the one she wants to capture, see her tasting his mouth again and see her tremble ever so quietly at the memory.

Why Meecha even bother, bother me, bother her? There's no use. But I know I have to go through it one more time, just in case, maybe this one will hear. I keep on.

"His hands. He had the most beautiful hands. Always clean nails and smooth on the inside. Big palms could hold my whole breast in one of them and just tease my nipples with his thumb.

"Well I didn't have as much up there then as I do now, child. I use to just watch him touch me like he was reading my body with his fingers, learning each place it turned or folded. He knew where to be soft and when to be firm, and I would get hotter and smoother and wetter as he slowly showed me he understood me and what I needed, what I wanted.

"He wasn't my first. Meecha always said I was too quick and too wild for my own good. I always answered, *What's a body for but to use.* I mean, I was honorable. But for me, respecting the body don't have nothing to do with keeping my knees locked together, and well I didn't have a need for marriage to tie me up and prevent me from taking my pleasure as a full-grown woman. I felt love was the only promise I needed. And I was loved.

"He would bring me presents too, sometimes a dried flower and sometimes some hot corn fritters. Did I tell you he could cook? Better than me, much better. I'm always in too much of a hurry. Don't want to take the time to make the foods let out their flavors. I've burnt many a pot bottom I can tell you. But he cooked without seeming to pay attention, always adding and stirring and turning the heat up or down just on time.

"During that time he lived with his brother officially, but his brother was gone home to Eleuthera where their people came from so we two had the house all to ourselves. We spent whole days rolling around with each other learning how we fit together, telling each other stories and lies and making love till the bed shook us off onto the floor, and then the floor disappeared and we're just panting and groaning and sweating and sighing and well..."

I pause.

It was a wonderful time, even with everything that had come and gone and rotted since then, it was a wonderful time.

"But you see child," I reach over and take her hand, "it wasn't really love; it was passion and lust and desire and need all tied together, but it wasn't love. It wasn't that pulling through the hard times and making sacrifices for each other and trying to knit together some kind of a life that is bigger than both of you. I thought it was love, but it wasn't. So, after a summer of looping the looping and drinking in each other's sweat and syrups and stretching and folding and collapsing inside and on top and underneath, indoors and in the open under a carpet of stars, he told me he was going off because he got a contract for work in another city. But I knew he'd be back soon enough. He promised to return, although he didn't say when, and he promised to write. And he did write, once. A pretty postcard he had made, with a photo of him working as a chef in one of those high-toned, big city restaurants. In the card, he promised to call me whenever he could. And he did call, twice.

"I missed him so much. The world went from being all bright orange and yellow to a gray-green. I stopped singing, hardly ate and just moped around. Meecha told me I was a fool. Said he had gone off with another girlfriend to work in her daddy's restaurant. I called her a liar and spat on her shadow. She laughed at me and offered me some magic dust to blow in the wind. She told me I could blow him away in the dust and not miss him one minute longer. But no, I wanted him back, and I was willing to put up with the pain of wanting him back. Meecha, she told me I had had him and should be thankful that I had more pleasure in one summer than some people have all their lives. She told me that now I had a standard and should not accept less loving than he gave me in the flesh, but next time to reach deeper through to the spirit. I told her she was crazy and didn't know about real love, talked about how she was always running off all the men who sniffed around her. I had love, real love, and she was jealous."

Unetha cuts in for the first time.

"What plans you two make for the future?"

"To love each other forever," I answer.

"That's what we say too. Say it every day. I mean every day we're together. Lately though, he's been a little busier. But we're going to love forever, I know it!"

"Yeah, well I knew it too, baby girl. That's what I told Meecha! But Meecha she just went on and screwed her mouth up at me. *Till there are no more stars*, she said real bitter.

"Yes," I answered, "till there are no more stars."

Unetha smiles to herself as she whispers, "Long as there is a bit of the sparkle of you in the winds or on the tip of a petal of a flower, as long as anyone anywhere remembers there ever was a you..."

Now I know this is definitely a waste of time, but I keep on.

"Unetha, there are going to be stars being born and stars dying forever, just like there are going to be men who say they'll love you till there are no more stars."

"Which means forever."

"That's what I said to Meecha, but she wouldn't hear it. Told me that she agreed, what he loved wasn't just getting between my young, strong legs. That maybe what he loved was holding my hand and playing house. But that he didn't have a hold of really loving a woman anywhere in his body. He only knew how to play at loving, pretend at giving.

"Well I walked away from Meecha and didn't talk to her for a whole week. It had only been Meecha and me since our parents died. Meecha, she never wanted children, and since she had raised me since I was seven, she felt she already had one. She always called me her sister-child. That's part of why my not talking to her really bothered her. You ever work with somebody and then go home to the same house with them and not talk for a whole week? Not a *good morning* or a *how you feeling* or an *excuse me*? I can hold water in my mouth. Always could.

But Meecha, it's hard for her. I knew what I was doing. I was wearing her down so that when I asked her for the second part of the spell, she'd do whatever needed to be done without any kind of hesitation. I wanted my man back."

"Sure enough when Christmas came, he returned to visit with his uncle and see his new baby cousin and to see me I thought, but he never had time for me. He was always in a hurry and kind of nervous. I went by his house and he welcomed me in, and we made love, but it was quick and careless. *I'm moving from here permanently*, he said, *I'm sorry but I just have to go.*

"I told him I'd come with him, but he told me it wasn't a good idea, said he'd send for me if he could, told me he still loved me although he looked out the door when he said he always would love me till all the stars fell from the sky. His words clanked onto the floor, and for a second or two, I thought they weren't real. But I pulled it together and realized that he was just hurting because he had to leave and go where he could make a better living for us. I made him promise, promise we could have one more night together before we left. And he agreed. *You know I can't resist your chocolate thighs and shimmering eyes. You make a fire in me.* And he kissed me and told me to meet him in two days.

"Well I ran home to Meecha and told her she just had to fix me the stew so he would stay. I begged and begged and begged and cried and carried on and she warned me again, told me that forever never stopped, that it meant every day not just till I died but from here through crossing over to wherever I was going after this life. Me and him, him and me. And I said that was no never mind to me. So, she made a stew and told me to feed it to him, but not eat but three bites myself.

"I went to his house that night with my casserole dish and a pie I had picked up and some makings for a salad. He was so pleased that I had brought dinner, and this time he was rushing to make love to me. But I didn't let him do anything but give me one long kiss. Meecha said don't let him inside me until he had eaten the food.

"So instead of letting him keep on, I sat him in a chair and then I unfolded a napkin and spread it on his lap, being careful to press his thigh and stroke him till I felt him swell under my touch, then I sat in his lap and wiggled my behind all tight on him and filled a fork with the stew thick with yams and chicken and slowly fed him. He chewed it slowly and smiled. *You cook this, Rhea?*

"I had some help," I said, and told myself I wasn't exactly lying. I peeled and chopped and stirred. I sorta helped to cook it. Maybe I was the help instead of getting it, but I was a part of making the meal. Literally a part of it since three drops of my blood was inside the meat.

"Well I fed him till he was full and only took three bites myself, and when I took my third bite I felt his arm sliding up under my blouse and he pulled me close like he used to do and breathed into my hair, *I missed your smell, and I missed these...* and he cradled my breasts and pulled my top over my head and I was sitting on him half-dressed and smiling at him. It looked like he found something he had lost. He stared at me so long and we spent a wonderful night together. But then come morning, he left anyway."

"I ran back to Meecha weeping, and she told me not to worry. He was mine. Forever. Well, sure enough, he came home six months later with a wife and seven-month-old baby in tow. Seemed that his uncle had a new business starting up and it was a good opportunity. Well, the first thing that man did, soon as he got his wife and baby settled was to come over to my house. I wanted to turn him away since he was married to someone else, but I couldn't. I loved him too much. So I let him come in. For two years we lived with him skulking in late at night and leaving before dawn.

"Then his wife threw a pot of boiled grits on him one night, stormed off with her child at her side, and went right on home to her daddy. I was glad. But you know, to tell the truth, by that time I was getting kind of tired of old Herman. I mean he was a good enough lover, but he didn't have nothing on his mind. And he had been married when I fed him that stew, already had a baby born and hadn't said a word to me, so he wasn't exactly an honest man, you know. And he just always wanted to be up under me, wouldn't give me no kinda space."

"Not like my man."

"Hrmmph. And he wasn't doing right by his child, and I just can't stand no man that doesn't do right by the babies he makes. And even though he worked, he didn't build. He was living in that same house and wasn't doing anything to make it nicer. He asked me to move in, and I did, but he wasn't about cooking for me like he used to. Oh, he cooked sometimes when he got a feeling for it, but mostly it was over-cooking or undercooking and him running off to this woman or that for a meal and some, but always coming back to me."

"Couldn't Meecha make it so he didn't look at any woman but you?"

"That was the next spell, and yeah I got that one too. She told me not to go there. Said there was a chance she could undo the first if I let him go because maybe someone else would want him like I did and that was the out, to pass the link on to her. But I was sure all our problems would go away if he just concentrated on me. And girl he did a mess of concentrating.

"He would be there in the morning, he would be there in the after-noon. Meecha and I had our shop by then, and he found a way to be there all the time. Oh, at first, he helped fix things nice, put up sheet-rock, painted, like that. But always kind of sullen about it. No joy, just like he had to do, had to be near, had to stay or else there was an ache inside him. That's how he explained it one night."

"So you still made love and..."

"Yes, and for a while it was great. I mean he had plenty of fire for me and I stayed satisfied."

"Sounds like heaven."

"He didn't see no one but me just like I asked for. I couldn't be with my friends without him complaining and moaning and groaning. I couldn't sit by myself without him wanting to at least be close and star-ing just staring and talking about how he'd love me till there were no fish in the sea. And I'd tell him to go to that sea and fish a few out so we could start on that road. I couldn't get him interested in anything, anything but me. It was like what used to be a fire, turned into a chain, and we were chained together."

"Did you have any children?"

"That was the worst. We made three babies, all girls. First was still-born, but I had Meecha make a potion the next time and that one, Corazon, she lived almost two years before she died in her sleep. And the last one was strangled by the umbilical cord. I asked her why they all died, and she reminded me there was always a price for what I asked."

"Would you have done it if you had known the price?"

"Can't know the price. It costs different for everyone. Herman held my hand through each of the funerals but didn't feel no loss. Said he couldn't feel anything but a fear that I would leave him one day. And he couldn't stand the pain if that happened, how he would never let that happen. And after a while, I didn't even want to lay up with him anymore. It kind of turned me that he wouldn't mourn for them."

"*Couldn't.*"

"At the time I didn't see it that way. But truth was, I didn't want him anymore. I outgrew him so to speak. So, I took up with Keho."

"The carver, that old man?"

"He wasn't old then, although he was older than me. And he was a kind man, a sure steady lover and real sensible. But he wouldn't ever let me spend the night, always sent me home to Herman. Told me that he'd make a home with me if I could get Herman out of my life. I told Herman to go away. Told him I didn't want him anymore. Kicked him out of the house he built. Sure did.

"And he left. Well sort of. He pitched a tent in the front and slept outside. He cried and asked me what he did wrong, begged me to let him back in, said he would love me till the snow melted off of all the mountains and the birds all stopped singing. And I told him I didn't want his boring, tired obsession, that it wasn't any kind of real love. That I couldn't use his stuck-to-me-like-some-super-glue-tearing-the-skin-offa-my-bones and he just whined and stayed like a whipped dog."

"Every morning I walked out my door there he'd be, every evening I came back in, there he'd be. Never got sick, never got tired, never stopped. I wanted something new, some kind of love for a grown woman. Was carrying Keho's son, my only child to live. Keho's fourth son. I was sure that would make Herman leave because he knew I hadn't let him up inside me in more than a year. But no, he just like a hungry, wet kitten.

"Finally, I let him come in because Keho had started acting stupid. He said he couldn't be around me with Herman hanging out like some kind of ghost. Said Herman was actually his godchild and that as a god-father, he had no business ever messing with me. Keho, he looked after his child after he was born, brought me money and soon as the boy was old enough to take care of his own toilet and wash himself proper, took the boy to stay with him much as he stayed with me. But we never could get it together, and I have never been able to keep a man since, except Herman that is."

There is a knock at the door. I ignore it.

"Want me to get it?"

"No child. It's Herman. Bringing me some damn flowers he stole from somebody's garden. I'll just leave them there and let them wilt. Baby, forever means forever. Always, it means always."

"Where's he live now?"

"Here, child. I just pushed him out the door this morning because I needed to be alone. He just stays around the back of the house and wait till the sun sets, and I let him back in."

"But just because it didn't work with Herman and you, that doesn't have anything to do with Lamont and me. Lamont, he reads and he wants to make the world a better place, he has lots of interests besides me. He just doesn't like to settle down."

"But if you make him go against his nature, child it'll turn him."

"Mama says every man only needs a good woman to make him settle down."

"Every man who is a settling man, but some men they ain't. You take what you can get from the others and then let them go. It's more than a notion to tie someone to you child."

"But you stopped loving your man. I'll never stop loving Lamont."

"No Unetha, there's a part of me still loves him. That's why I let him back in all the time. But you know, after a while his caresses got the same because he really wanted to leave, but he just couldn't. And I got careless in my loving because I wanted him to go, but he wouldn't."

"*Couldn't.*"

"You a bright one. Yes, couldn't. See he couldn't do anything really new or adventurous because it would have cracked the spell of staying. I had locked our love up in a piece of granite, and sure enough it was not going anywhere, but it couldn't grow and change, and thin and thicken, and tear like love is supposed to do. Instead, it petrified and grew heavy and gray. If I had just let knowing him be enough, if I had let him pass through my life, I'd had a better time. Instead, I got a hangdog man haunting my doorstep, walking down the road with me FOREVER! Yeah with the help of Meecha's spells I can always keep him several feet away. But after the sun sets, he comes back around with his foolish grin and empty mind. He's mine all mine cause no one else wants him. And me, I don't really want him either no more neither. But he's mine forever. Forever, child."

"It doesn't have to be that way."

"You ever go to the zoo, baby?"

"I don't much like the zoo. Caging animals like that."

"Then why you want to say you love someone and put them in a cage?"

She sits up all insulted. "Loving me is not the same as being locked up in a cage."

"You can't make a spell to have someone love you, sweetie. You can only make them stay."

"But he already loves me. And if he stays, he'll have to love me even more because I love him so much."

"No child, he'll just have to stay. Free love is the only love baby. Free to give, free to receive. No candles, no herbs, no guarantees."

"Some men don't have the sense to love who they are supposed to. What's so wrong with helping them out a little?"

"Child, a man who don't have the sense to love you with all you bring, don't have sense. Let it go."

She gets up and smiles. "I thank you for your time and your advice. Meecha told me to think on it two weeks and then come back to her or not, as I thought was best. I'll think on it."

I walk her to the door. When I open it, there is Herman standing at the bottom of the stairs.

"Herman, Unetha. Unetha, Herman." I introduce them and turn my back to Herman before he can say a word to me. I notice the jar of flowers sitting in front of my door and resist the impulse to just kick them over. It would be like kicking a mangy old dog, so I let them stay.

I hear him talking to Unetha as I shut the door.

"I love that woman, gonna love her till there's no more water in the rivers, till the sun dries up all the corn. I tell you..."

As I look out the window, I see Unetha smiling and shaking her head and walking fast as she can, trying to get away. Or maybe she is rushing to that Lamont of hers, can't really tell. Maybe she heard me and won't go back up to Meecha for that potion.

If so she'd be the first one who never did, the very first one.

Up North

The summer before I went to fifth grade, me and my mama moved to an all-white neighborhood in Philadelphia, Pennsylvania. I didn't want to leave the South, but she got a new job as a housekeeper for some rich white folks. My great aunt Edna worked for them first, and before she died, she told Mr. Sutherland all about Mama and her strong work ethic. He trusted Aunt Edna's judgment, so he sent for her immediately. He offered her what must've been a lot of money back then because she had us all packed up and on the road in less than three days. She said it would be better living in the North, but I couldn't imagine life much sweeter than where I came from. Aiken, South Carolina.

I was sure up North I wasn't gonna be able to walk barefoot outside and feel the grass and dirt graze the soles of my feet. I wasn't going to be able to run out of the house just in time to catch Mr. Leonard strolling by with his fruit cart. I'd always wake up extra early to catch him before anyone else did. Early mornings were the only time he had the fattest peaches with the fuzziest skin, they were my favorite. I loved sitting under the big sycamore trees for shade, eating those peaches and letting the juice run down my chin and neck. When I was good and sticky, I would run over to the pond and rub the cool water on my hands, face, and neck. Some mornings I would even stop to listen to birds. Listen to the trees wrestling with the wind. Other mornings, I wouldn't listen for anything. I would just stand there in the pond staring up at the sky, trying to see if my eyes could make new shapes with the clouds. This was my summertime ritual, as Mama would say. She said she never interrupted me because she knew it was personal time that me and God needed to have.

"For years coloreds been moving up North for more money, and maybe I was too afraid before, but I'm ready now." I heard Mama talkin' to Mr. Rich days before we left. Mr. Rich had been sweet on her for years. She always told him that she was too busy to be foolin' around with him. But I saw him come in one night when she thought I was asleep. It was a school night, and company wasn't allowed on a school night. But there he was, tiptoeing on the creaking floorboards, so I know she was just as sweet for him as he was for her.

"Bea, I make enough money to take care of all of us. Savannah won't need a thing. You won't need a thing. C'mon just stay."

I watched Mama and Mr. Rich from a distance. I didn't want to interrupt, and I didn't want them to think I was eavesdropping. She always said my curious eyes and ears were gonna get me in some serious trouble one day.

"Just stop it Rich, you know I can't let you take care of all of us. I just gotta go to see what's up there. Anything gotta be betta than what me and Savannah got here."

Mama looked around at the small kitchen they sat in. I didn't think it was so bad. There was a leak in the faucet that Mr. Rich had to patch up every other week, and we had to have plastic covering the windows in the winter months. Sometimes the stove quit working, but Mr. Rich fixed it every time. He always did work around the house for us, because I never had a daddy to help. Well, Mama said I had a daddy once, but I was too young to remember him. When I was a baby, he left to go to work and never came back. We were never sad about it. We just learned to live without him. For me that was easy, because I never knew him. Not much to show for him ever being around. I had one flimsy old picture of him and Mama when they first met. They were smiling with their arms wrapped around each other. I could see that her heart was lighter back then. She never smiled like that anymore.

The morning of our trip came fast. I didn't have time to grab peaches from Mr. Leonard the night before, so I was hoping to catch him that morning. I didn't think they would have peaches in the North so I needed to get as many as I could. Mama told me that we didn't have time to waste. We had to be in Pennsylvania by the time the sun set, because traveling the night roads could be dangerous for a Black mama and her Black daughter.

"Mama?"

She looked at me in the rearview mirror waiting for me to go on.

"Why didn't you let me get my peaches?

She paused for a second before turning down the radio.

"Savannah, you can get some peaches when we get up North. We don't have time to be sittin' around waitin' for no peaches."

"How you know they got peaches up North, Mama? We ain't never been before, we don't know what they got." I folded my arms across my chest.

"Child, you'll get some peaches and some other fruits. Don't worry." She rolled her eyes and threw her hand up to shoo away my thoughts. "And you best unfold them arms, Savannah, 'less you want your lips popped!'"

"Well, why we have to rush anyway?" I slowly unfolded my arms because I didn't wanna challenge her threat.

"Told you I wanna get there by sunset. It's dangerous to ride through certain parts at night. Them Klan boys get a hold of you and that's it. They'll kill you right on the spot."

For a while, we didn't say much. I guess we both just wanted to make it there safely. I wondered what life was gonna be like for us.

"You ever saw one before?"

"One of what?"

"A Klan boy."

She waited a few seconds before answering. "Once when I's about your age." She shook her head at the memory like she was trying to erase it.

"What'd they do to you?"

"Nothing. My daddy wouldn't let them hurt me. We were on a long road trip just like this one, and we somehow got lost so Daddy stopped at a store to ask for directions. The clerk, a white man, was givin' him all types of crazy instructions. Tellin' him things like 'go up this hill and keep goin' till you reach a shack.' Didn't sound right, but we didn't know what else to do since we was lost. It was dark, and Daddy was so tired. Once Daddy finished with the man, we went in the snack aisle to find something wit a little sugar in it. Somethin' to keep us awake and alert, and sure enough this old Black man come outta nowhere tellin' us to go back the way we came. Whispered in Daddy's ear tellin' him the Klan stay up them hills by that shack, and that clerk was a Klan member too. I swear that man musta been some kinda angel."

"You wouldn't let them take me, right Mama?"

"Savannah, I wouldn't let nothing take you from me."

We were both quiet for a while until she broke the silence by turning the radio back up.

Somewhere between down South and up North, I fell asleep.

When I woke up, we were arriving in Gladwyne, Pennsylvania. There were no coloreds in sight. No colored little girls playing hopscotch or hand games in the streets. No colored mamas hanging sheets on the clothesline to dry. No colored brothers rolling dice in the alley. In fact, there were no alleys. No lingering trash that usually accompanied the alleys. There was nothing but green trees, swaying and twirling with clean air. Even the sky seemed to be a little bluer. The sun, brighter. I didn't like it.

"Mama, where are all the colored people?"

"Ain't none. We the only colored folk you gonna see," she replied with a slight shrug of her shoulders.

We were driving down a long road and my eyes were fixed on the lines turning from dotted to solid. We never had white painted lines in the South. It was mostly just dirt roads. I watched her wide eyes in the rearview mirror. She looked nervous or scared. But I couldn't tell what had her so uneasy. This was the same woman who brought a six-footer down to his knees because he called her an ugly nigger. I thought she was gonna kill him until Mr. Rich pulled her off. I never saw a white man run so fast.

Mama would go out in the yard every day and wrestle with hogs and chickens until they became dinner on our plates. She wasn't no small woman. She stood five feet eleven inches and had wide hips that bounced and rocked as she walked. *Left. Right. Left. Right.* If you got in the way as she was walking, them hips would knock you over into yesterday. One day I was walking up under her and I got too close. Her hips got to swinging, and I got caught in the crossfire. I flew into the wall so hard that I had a knot on the side of my head for days after.

Her feet were long and thick. Her soles were hard because she never wore shoes in the yard. She always said that shoes got in the way of her yard work. She loved to feel the dirt collect around her bare feet. The soil kept her cool on hot days.

"You heard the story 'bout that Till boy that got killed a few years back?" She raised her eyebrow at me to make sure I was listening. "All because he wanted to show off. Be big time. I know you like to talk to people and make friends, but you mind your eyes and your business 'round these white folks."

"Wasn't that in Mississippi somewhere?"

"Don't matter where it was. It could happen to you too if you don't act right. White folks always wanna make an example outta coloreds. Always wanna get rid of us some kind of way. You hear me, child?"

"Yes, Mama. I'll mind my ways here. Won't get in nobody else's way either."

Mama made sure that I knew what I was and what it meant to be me. She always reminded me of the little bit of rights that colored people had. Told me to never look white people in the eyes. She said I could never be too brave or they would hang me. Can't be too loud or they would beat me. Can't ever be proud, or surely I would die. Can't be alone because them older white boys would rape me. As a Black girl, all I was supposed to know was how to clean up 'round the house, and put food on the table.

I didn't know what color I was until I came in the house one day upset and crying.

"Mama, I had to beat Sammy up today." I fell on the couch and buried my five-year-old face in my hands. Sammy was my best friend. A white girl with red hair and freckles that matched. She came from a poor family. They lived about two miles down the road from us.

"What you mean you beat her up? Don't be goin' around here causin' no trouble, Savannah. What happened?"

"Well, she called me black."

"So why would that get you all upset?"

"I'm not black, Mama."

"Oh really? Well what color are you?"

I ran back to her room and returned with her small stuffed doll that her grandmother had sewn for her when she was a little girl. The doll was jet black with two big white eyes. Her hair was made from black yarn, and her lips were tightly sewn into a pink smile.

"See Mama! This is black." I held the doll to my arm and compared the colors. "I'm brown, Mama. Not black."

She chuckled and explained to me what it meant for someone to call me black. She remembered having a conversation with her Nana about why the doll didn't look like her. Her nana explained that the stores didn't have any brown material to make dolls.

"It don't mean you black like that doll, Savannah. Just like white people ain't white like milk. Just the way it is."

The next day she made me apologize to Sammy and invited her over for dinner.

"So what we gonna do when we get there, Mama?" I was afraid I wouldn't make any friends if she didn't let me show myself to anyone.

"I'm gonna have some work to do so I need you to sit and be quiet."

We pulled in front of a big white house with balconies on all three levels. The shutters were dark green. On the porch was a long swinging chair that a little girl sat in.

"Don't you say nothing 'less I tell you to speak, hear?" She pointed her finger at me.

"Yes, Mama." I lowered my head.

I pouted as we walked up to the porch until she shot me a look that told me to straighten up right away unless I wanted to get popped on my lips. She would do that sometimes if she thought I was pouting for no reason. She told me it was so my lips wouldn't get stuck that way.

The girl jumped from the swing and threw her arms out to catch her balance. She laughed.

"Hi. I'm Cindy Sutherland, and this is my daddy's house."

She was my height and looked me straight in the eyes. She had one green eye, and the other was blue. I had never met anyone with two different colored eyes before. Her hair was gold and curly like the white girls you see in the fairy tale books. She had on a blue dress with white ruffles on the arms. I looked at my brown shirt and mustard yellow corduroy jumper and felt ashamed. I wanted to have a dress with ruffles, but the only time I got to wear a dress was for church, and it wasn't half as pretty as hers.

Cindy held out her hand, and I looked at Mama and waited for her to tell me it was okay to shake it. She nodded.

"Hi. I'm Savannah, and this is my mama."

Her hand was soft, and she smelled like cotton candy.

"Pleased to meet you," Cindy said. "You must be my new caretaker! Edna told me all about you before she got sick. I sure do miss her a lot."

Her smile disappeared.

Mama placed her hand on Cindy's shoulder and smiled.

"I miss her too, but don't you worry, honey. I'm gonna take good care of you. I learned everything from her."

I wondered why she never called *me* honey.

Cindy smiled. Her teeth were small, white, and all in one straight line in her mouth. "What do I call you?"

"Just call me Bea, short for Beatrice."

Mama grabbed my hand and Cindy's hand and took us into the house.

"Well, I see you've met our sweet little Cindy girl," Mrs. Sutherland said. She was a petite woman with dark brown hair. Her waist was much smaller than Mama's. She wore a bright yellow skirt and a white shirt with pearl-colored buttons that was tucked tightly.

"Yes. She is quite a doll," Mama said as she shook Mrs. Sutherland's hand. I had never heard her use the word 'quite' before. It made me feel weird.

"Edna was such a lovely woman. We sure are gonna miss her around here. But she spoke so highly of you, we knew that we needed to have you right away."

Mama smiled.

"Hello, Bea! So glad to see you've made it." Mr. Sutherland was stepping lightly down each step on the spiral staircase. His pants were dark gray, and his shirt was white with black buttons. A black untied tie was draped around his neck. Mama told me that Mr. Sutherland was a very wealthy man. He was the owner of one of the largest furniture stores in the state of Pennsylvania. "And you must be darling little Savannah!" He opened his palm and reached his arm toward me.

I shook his hand and looked down to the ground. I was too afraid to look him in the eye, especially after Mama told me not to do that.

"Nice to meet you, Mr. Sutherland. Thank you for having us here." I repeated Mama's words like a record player.

"Savannah, we're family now. Call me Uncle Don."

I was surprised at how friendly he was. Mama always said that rich white folk wasn't friendly.

That night, she cooked us a big dinner. She said it was her Southern specialty, but wasn't nothing special about it. It was the same thing she made for me all the time back at home. Fried smothered pork chops, collard greens soaked in fatback, mac and cheese, yams, and peach cobbler with ice cream for dessert. Peach cobbler was my favorite.

Mama was so different around the Sutherlands. She kept her hair pressed and tied neatly into a bun. She even started putting blue ribbons around the bun. She started talking funny. She said it was polite to use good English around the Sutherlands. I got dizzy from watching her tongue twist and curl to form good English. I don't think the Sutherlands even noticed.

The Sutherlands were very nice, but very busy. They were almost never home. Every time I saw them, they were either coming or going. They would give me and Cindy a quick wave or pat on the head before leaving.

"Play nice, girls," Mrs. Sutherland would say with a slight smirk.

Cindy and I played all summer long.

"Now Ms. Savannah, when you go to that big, important job you can have shiny shoes." Cindy laughed as she pretended to polish my imaginary business shoes. She loved her own imagination, and so did I. She made me think that I could do things that Mama would never agree with.

Cindy threw one of Mr. Sutherland's suit jackets around my shoulders. "Mrs. President," she said with her chest full of pride.

"Yes, Secretary of State? What can I help you with?" I replied through my hand, trying to keep the giggles from escaping my mouth.

"You have a busy day. You have to save the whole world." Cindy held her arms out as wide as they would stretch. "That's a lot of work! Should I get you some coffee?"

"Absolutely," I said in the same high-pitched tone I heard Mama use when she wanted to please Mrs. Sutherland.

"How do you want your coffee, Mrs. President?"

"All black with a little sugar in it, please."

"Coming right up." Cindy high stepped out of the room and returned, saying that we had to pause our pretend because Mama wanted us to take our baths.

Mama came in the bathroom while I was bathing and sat at the edge of the tub. She carried the same expression on her face the night she told me that we were moving. I thought that maybe she was about to change her mind about being here.

"Savannah," she started with a heavy sigh, "are you having a good time here?"

"Of course, Mama. I love it. Cindy's my best friend."

She grabbed the washcloth and began to scrub my back.

"Now I know you havin' fun and all, but don't forget the things I told you."

"I know Mama, but it's just pretend."

"It's fine to play pretend, Savannah, but you won't ever be able to do those things. Don't think I don't hear y'all when Cindy makes you play the parts of Presidents and business people. Little Black girls like you don't do things like that. You understand me?"

"Yes Mama, I know."

She gave me back the washcloth and walked out of the bathroom. I knew she was right. She had been telling me these things since I was old enough to understand.

I looked at my skin and, for the first time, I hated the brown that covered my body. I felt my hair and tried to get my fingers through the tangles, but my hands got stuck. I closed my eyes and wished for swinging, golden curls like Cindy. I'd even take her two different colored eyes. I wanted her sweet-smelling skin dotted in light brown freckles. Only then could I be all those things I pretended to be.

I cried myself to sleep that night.

"Princesses and maids, Savannah! Time to get up and play." Cindy jumped all over me and pulled me out of the bed. "You sure are sleepy this morning, can't spend all day sleeping!"

I didn't tell Cindy that I spent all night trying to soothe myself because Mama wouldn't do it for me. She wasn't the type of woman to wipe my tears away or rub my head when I had a headache. I had to learn to do it on my own, because that's the only way I was gonna grow to be strong. I hopped out of bed and ran to our playroom.

The playroom was big and bright pink. Cindy had all types of costumes and baby dolls and teddy bears. There was a tea set that we only used on special occasions. This is where we spent the most time pretending that I was things I could never be in real life.

"I'm supposed to be the maid, Cindy!" I started to get upset because she wasn't playing fair. "I've never seen a white maid before. Only Black ones."

"Well, maybe we can change it just for pretend. Don't you wanna be a princess for a little while? You can wear my princess tiara."

"Cindy, you gotta have long hair to be a princess. Long hair that moves when you walk. My hair don't do that."

"Savannah, that's not true. Besides this is our game and we make our own rules. Our kind of princesses can have short hair."

"But you have long hair, and it's pretty." I sighed.

"I'll be back!" Savannah left, and I sat down to think about how it would feel to be a princess in the game. A Black princess with nappy hair. Wouldn't nobody want me as their princess.

"Look, Savannah! Now you can be the princess because your hair is longer than mine."

I turned around to see Cindy with her gold curls dangling in her hand. Her hair was so short that if it weren't for her pretty dress and white ruffled socks, I would've sworn she was a boy. My mouth was wide open, and I didn't realize it till she came over and nudged my chin to help me close it.

Cindy didn't say anything, she just sat at the foot of the bed and put my foot in her lap, and pretended to shine my shoes again. "Little brown girl, you'll grow to do wonderful things. You'll be somebody's princess," Cindy said with a smile, while rubbing my feet.

"Cindy Sutherland, get your hind parts down these steps!" I heard Mama call out in a nervous tone. "You too, Savannah!"

We ran down the steps to see her holding a napkin full of Cindy's hair that she had gathered from the sink. Her hand covered her mouth when she saw Cindy.

"Child, what have you done! Mrs. Sutherland is gonna have a fit when she sees this."

"Well, I didn't want Savannah to feel bad because her hair isn't as long as mine."

Mrs. Sutherland walked in. The bags that she dropped were now at her feet with items pouring out of them. "Cindy, my goodness. What in the world have you done to your hair?"

"I just wanted the game to be fair, Mommy. I didn't want Savannah to be sad."

"You and Savannah get upstairs right now, and let me and Bea have a talk." Mrs. Sutherland dismissed us without looking at me.

We sat at the top of the steps and listened to Mama and Mrs. Sutherland.

"Bea, I don't know how much longer we can do this. I really like you being here and you're such a big help, but I need someone who's gonna watch the girls. Cindy should not have been allowed to cut her hair. What are my friends going to think? Where were you?"

"I-I'm sorry, Mrs. Sutherland. You know how those girls get to runnin' 'round this house and half the time ya can't find them. I'll be sure to take better care of them. Don't worry at all about Cindy's hair. Edna taught me a good home remedy to make it grow back real fast. All I gotta do is grab some fish oil from the market. Give it two weeks; it'll be longer than it was before."

"Bea, I just don't think that it's a good idea to have them around each other all the time. I just think that maybe they need a break from each other."

"What are you trying to say, Mrs. Sutherland?"

"I'm saying that I think Savannah is a nice girl, but Cindy has a very active imagination and it's not good for her to have a friend around and no one to watch them."

When we heard Mama walking up the steps, we ran to Cindy's room and pretended to play with her dollhouse. I felt guilty. Even though Cindy was the one that cut her own hair, I knew it wasn't right. Now Mama was gettin' in trouble because of me.

"What are you girls up to?" She came in the room with her hands on her hips. She smiled softly. "Savannah come here for a moment. I need your help in the kitchen."

I followed her to the kitchen. She didn't look happy, but she didn't look upset either. She had a pitiful look in her eyes.

"I think you and Cindy have been spendin' too much time together, and she's fillin' your head with all that nonsense. I already told you Black children don't grow up to be nobody's Presidents or have maids, and you got her runnin' 'round here choppin' all her hair off. Her mama sayin' that you a bad influence on her."

"Mama we just pretendin', I know I can't be those things, but it's nice to act like it's okay sometimes. I told her that we can't play like this 'round other people and she said it was okay 'cause it's just me and her."

"Look, honey. I really need this job. These people payin' me good money to stay here and help them out. I was talkin' to Rich today, and he thinks that you should come home and stay with him. You know he could use your help around the yard and he would love to have you home again."

"You don't want me here with you?" I could feel my throat gettin' tight and sore. I didn't wanna leave. I loved this place. I loved Cindy. But I knew that Mama needed this job and I couldn't be upset. Mama was always saying I gotta grow up sooner than I would ever want to because I'll be faced with problems like that.

She didn't let me say goodbye to Cindy because she thought it would be too hard for me, but I think it would've been too hard for her.

Mr. Rich met Mama half way to pick me up the next morning. When he got out of the car, he walked up to her and gave her a long hug. He whispered something in her ear and Mama buried her face in his chest. I don't know what Mr. Rich said, but it was nice to see Mama being so soft with him. He gave me a strong hug, a light smile, and a pat on the head. I missed him in the way I imagined little girls miss their fathers.

Mama placed her hands on my shoulders.

"Now you be good, Savannah, I don't wanna hear no mess 'bout how you showin' off and actin' like God ain't give you no good sense." Mama pointed her finger at me, pulling me in for a hug.

"Yes, Mama," I said with my head toward the ground. I had my eyes fixed on my white, patent leather shoes, Cindy's hand-me-downs. "I'll behave."

Mama hugged me even tighter.

"I know in this life you barely get what you want, but God always gives you what you need."

The ride home was quiet. There wasn't much to say. Mr. Rich tried to make conversation, but I wasn't in the mood for small talk. I wasn't sure exactly how I felt. I knew I missed Cindy, but I knew I didn't belong up North with her. I knew I missed Sammy, but I felt like I didn't belong down South with her either.

I awoke at the sound of Mr. Rich beeping his horn as we were riding by Sammy's house.

"Sammy said to let her know as soon as we got back. She can't wait to see you!" He was more excited than I was about our reunion.

We pulled up to the house, and it was exactly the same as when I had left. Small, pleasant, and falling apart. I could tell that Mr. Rich tried to make it feel like home. He planted some flowers and small plants in the front yard. It was nice.

I turned around to see Sammy running toward me, smiling and waving a peach in the air. I almost forgot about Mr. Leonard's sweet peaches. She ran to me with her arms as wide as they could stretch and gave me the biggest hug I'd ever had. She felt like home. Sammy reminded me of the backyard pond that I rinsed myself in, and the dirt roads that I had walked along with bare feet. I felt my heart lighten.

She smelled like pine wood that had been soaking in the rain. Her overalls were loose and covered in a light layer of dirt. I wondered if that's what I looked like the first time Cindy saw me.

I had on one of Cindy's old dresses and a ribbon in my hair. Sammy stepped back and tugged on the dress and made a face as if something rotten was near. I could tell that she didn't like it, but she wouldn't say anything about it.

"I went to see Mr. Leonard bright and early this morning. I made sure I got the juiciest peach for you!" Sammy tossed the peach into my hands.

I took a huge bite, and juice ran down to my neckline, staining my collar.

"So you gonna take that dress off anytime soon?" Sammy smirked.

"Nope. I think I'll keep it on for a while."

I took one last bite out of my peach and buried the seed in the dirt. I sat on the ground, pulled off my white shoes and tossed them aside. I gave myself a moment to feel the South's dirt between my toes.

When I stood up, I noticed that my dress was covered in dirt. Sammy laughed.

"Wanna go play in the pond?" I asked.

"But your dress!"

"This ain't no place for pretty white dresses, Sammy."

I ran toward the pond and Sammy followed. I stood in the water and let it cleanse me.

"Get all that North off of you." Sammy laughed.

Aiken was my home, and no life up North could ever be as sweet as this place.

Mary, Mara, and Death

Mary Chapman

I wished to be a flower child. Dancing and music, drugs and sex. My dream was to create a commune that had at least one person from every race on this earth. At the age of eight, I knew without a doubt that I hated the institution of marriage and swore I would love freely. None of my ten children would know who fathered them. I would name each of them after flowers, boy or girl. Everyone in my commune would be mothers and fathers to my children. We would all love each other, and that would be enough.

But I was a good Christian girl named Mary who went to her parents' Baptist church every Wednesday and Sunday. Who babysat kids in the neighborhood after school while their parents finished up their shifts and came home for a few hours before their graveyard shifts started. My momma worked two jobs, so she'd come home at 7 PM and check in on us. I'd watch multiple kids at a time at my house. I'd call them sleepovers, and I'd have the kids hold hands like I saw Dr. King do and we'd all sing spirituals while walking around the house. Sometimes, I'd stand on my bed and say as much of the "I Have A Dream" speech as I could remember. I'd quiver my voice just like him. All the kids, young and with boogers hanging from their noses, would look up at me enraptured.

In 1975, I was 15 and desperate to dance. I wanted to feel the passionate desperation of the unfulfilled dream from Dr. King's speech on that dance floor, mixed with coke and body sweat all squeezed into a brightly colored skin-tight, bell-bottomed jumpsuit. I wanted to snort so much coke I couldn't feel my face.

In 1978, I was finally old enough to run off to college and burn my bra. I had missed the chance to jump onto a smoke-filled rainbow-colored bus or to become the next Donna Summer, but I would find my rebellion. Then my father died. My mother had no one and needed to make up for the lost income from the two jobs my father worked. So I got a waitressing job and settled for wearing a fro and my uniform without a bra.

At night, I would search out disco clubs still barely holding on. Hole in the walls with floors that only partially lit up, believing despite the obvious truth, that disco would live forever. I'd sit at the bar and watch the few people still willing to stuff themselves into tight-fitting body and pant suits sweat out the cocaine in their systems. I was too afraid to dance. I'd practice at home while listening to Donna Summer and Gloria Gaynor on Momma's big wooden record player. But I felt apart from them sitting on a worn leather swivel stool with padding coming out of the bottom. I had missed this boat as well. I would never understand the euphoria of being part of a whole.

I'd generally wait for some drunk idiot to strut up to me in a polyester suit. The more ridiculous the strut, the quicker I'd bed them. Then I was thirty. It was 1990 and I was still working at the diner. My biggest form of revolt was still not wearing a bra. I had cut my fro short and started wearing bands in front of it so that it was styled.

On a particularly slow day at the diner, I decided to buy myself a pie. I sat at the counter and dug into it with a spoon. Rain started to come pouring down. I turned around on the stool to watch people run. Then he walked in. A Black cowboy, I swear to God. He strutted in soaking wet. He stood just in the doorway and took his hat off his head and brought it to his chest as he bowed his head to me. Then he walked right to a booth and slid in. No rush. No hurry. I put the spoon I was holding with a heaping mound of cherry pie down and took the pie pan back to the back. I straightened the scarf at my neck and pulled my shirt straight. Then I ran back out and asked him what he wanted. He asked if I didn't mind bringin' that pie back 'round. Just like that. I grinned, and brought the pie back out and slid into the booth across from him.

We ate my pie. I laughed out loud at the thought and told him aloud what I was thinking. He blushed, and I realized he was a gentleman and I'd love this man for the rest of my life. And I did, but in the meantime, I burst through the door of my house that night and Hustled down the hallway and Funky Chickened around the living room.

My momma jumped up and, beaming, turned on KC and The Sunshine Band, and we did The Bump until she had to stop. Then she turned me around and squeezed me, "Who is it dovey?"

And I smiled big. "His name is Ezekial."

Momma smiled even bigger. "God strengthens. Praise God, a good Christian man!"

In that moment, I hesitated. This was nothing like the hippie commune I had dreamed of as a girl. But then my momma was grabbing my arms and doing The Hustle, and I couldn't disappoint her.

Ez met my momma on a Tuesday night. She just about lost her mind when he took off his stetson for her as well. My daddy had been a man of the church, but men just weren't made like him anymore, I was a lucky girl to have found him. And when he asked her for my hand a month later, she said yes, and so did I.

We married at the Baptist church down by my cousin's house in Georgia, where my parents married. He waited for me at the altar still damp and smelling of the creek behind the church. He believed a man was only a man if he was willing to embrace every part of the woman he loved, so before the ceremony, he was baptized.

Then I was pregnant and we were moving to a tiny two-bedroom house in front of a field in Suffolk. Ez told me he wanted to grow an apple orchard. I laughed, thinking it was a joke, and I told him as well. I said, "I thought you were a cowboy."

He lifted his hat and sat it back on his head, but further back than before. There was no mistaking the passion in his eyes, "No ma'am, I'm a gardener."

I asked, "Doesn't it take a few years for the trees to get big enough to bear fruit?"

He smiled. "I waited for you, love."

I sighed. Of course more waiting.

While we waited, my cowboy husband worked as a short order cook at three diners. Ez would come home around midnight with leftovers from his last job of the day and pass out until 4 AM. Then he'd get up and sit at the table while I made him breakfast. He'd tease me, saying my face was too serious for no reason. I'd exaggerate the face, and he'd kiss me on the side of my neck. "Your face will get stuck like that, wife."

Our daughter Mara, who we called Little Ma, teethed, lost her baby teeth, got chickenpox, and started singing in the kids' choir at church.

My momma sold her house, moved down to Georgia, moved back up to Virginia and shared a room with Little Ma, then moved to a retirement home because she thought our tiny two-bedroom was a bit tight.

Then it was 1995, and Little Ma was getting ready to start kindergarten. I was excited. I'd finally get time to figure myself out. I hadn't dreamed of anything but apple trees, the church, my momma, and Little Ma. Things would be good.

I sat at my kitchen table drinking instant coffee and eating bacon when I saw a flash of light out of the window. I walked outside barefoot and curious, and there on a tree hung a bright, juicy, red apple. I reached up and pulled it down. I looked all around it, and there were no blemishes or holes where a hungry worm might have eaten its way through. I didn't take it in to wash it, I simply bit into it, trusting nature. The juice from the apple ran down the sides of my mouth, sweet and a bit tart, and I got it. My cowboy's patience. I decided I would go back to college and get my teaching certificate like I had planned to do eighteen years ago. I signed up for classes. I bought my books, a backpack, notebooks, and pens. Ez chuckled deep and rumbling as he watched me flit around getting everything ready. He said he had never seen me so excited. He sat at the kitchen table comfortably. He had quit his morning job so he could tend to his trees now that they were bearing fruit.

He put a cigarette in his mouth and lit it up and pulled on it. Then balanced it in his mouth as he drank his black coffee. Then he reached into his back pocket and pulled out his wallet. He handed me two hundred dollars and told me he had saved this money so I could buy some new clothes and shoes. Little Ma came into the kitchen, ready for me to walk her to school, but I was too excited. I jumped up and picked her up and swung her around. Then I put her down and taught her the moves to The Hustle and Ez sat back in his chair with the cigarette still in his mouth, and he laughed and laughed.

Little Ma ran outside to the orchard and I chased after her. She stopped, breathless, in the middle of the trees and started doing The Hustle to no music at all. I sang and did an exaggerated version of the dance and Little Ma did the same, only stopping to hold her sides as she laughed. Ez came out of the back door with the kitchen table and then I started to laugh too. He carried the table out to the middle of the trees where we were. Me and Little Ma ran for the chairs. Then we sat outside mid-morning in the middle of our orchard smiling crazy at each other because we had all decided to skip out on everything we had planned to do that day. Then Little Ma jumped up and started singing *Hot Stuff* while Hustling around the orchard. I got up to join her but found myself winded, so I sat back down and watched our little girl twirl and sing and dream.

The next day I couldn't get out of bed. I felt like I had the flu. I blamed it on the shoeless outdoor dancing the night before, but after two weeks Ez drove me to the hospital. After a biopsy and more waiting, they told me I had stage four breast cancer that had spread to my lymph nodes and my lungs. There was nothing they could do but give me the contact information for the local hospice and give me painkillers. I went home.

It felt like I had missed my chance again. I sat at the breakfast table alone, Ez decided to go back to his morning job so he could pay for my medical bills. He had also decided to move the breakfast table back inside so I wouldn't catch a chill, which I laughed at.

But sitting inside at the table looking out at those apples, I decided I still had a choice. So I took the money Ez had saved for me and bought the cheapest cruise I could find. It was a 70s revival two-night cruise on the Chesapeake Bay.

That night I told Ez I didn't want Little Ma to remember me shriveled and bald. He held his forehead against mine, his hands held tight to my hands. He didn't say a word. He breathed in and out three times, then he let me go, turned and walked into our bedroom and closed the door.

I didn't say goodbye to Little Ma.

Momma insisted on coming on the cruise with me. I told her to come collect my body. She asked how I knew God was ready to take me. I told her God had nothing to do with this. This was finally about me. She looked up at me, getting my meaning. It made her an old woman, the realization. She seemed to cave into herself. Her face sagged and wrinkled. I detected hints of grey at her roots. She fingered the cross at her neck. Then she sighed. It was never-ending.

I stood with her, allowing her her time. Then I reached out for her hands, the way she used to when I fell and needed comfort. I leaned down and kissed my momma's forehead. I told her I loved her. She nodded, a child consoling herself. Then she grasped my hands tight, squeezing tighter and tighter, trying to convince my body to live. Pleading. I stood quietly, patiently. Resolved. She released me. I turned and walked away quickly, so she wouldn't think I had changed my mind.

When I reached the end of the hallway, I turned around for one last wave. She stood, watching me walk away; her hand raised and her other arm supporting the raised arm as if it was taking all of her to do this one simple action. I waved and turned away and walked out of the door.

I chose a gold-colored rented bodysuit to die in. It was skin tight. I figured they wouldn't take it back after. I spent an hour blowing and picking out my fro, so that it was just right, though I knew I would lie on it and ruin the back of it. I wore matching gold platform shoes, also rented. Tonight I'd be seen, and it would be impossible to dethrone me. I took the bottle of pills before I went out so I didn't have to wait around in my room to die. I was tired of waiting.

My last meal was lobster. I soaked each bite in butter. I drank a bottle of Italian wine on the side. It was sweet and I drank it like juice. I ordered three pieces of apple pie for dessert.

I was ready.

I strutted to the dance club. Didn't look a single person in the eyes, because I was queen and would be until I dropped dead. I walked onto that floor with all eyes on me, and I started to Hustle. I twirled and gyrated. Then it didn't matter what I did, and my body moved to no discernible pattern at all. Sweat cascaded down. I couldn't feel my lips. They were numb. This was my moment. My arms flailed. My feet stamped. My hips moved side to side. Nothing else mattered.

Mara Maybelle Chapman

Mara sits in the stark white hospital room. She sits in a canvas chair next to a bed that takes up most of the room. Her dad lays in the bed, prone. His arms placed on top of the folded over sheet and blanket on top of him. His face is slack, relaxed, but to Mara already looking like death. Mara reaches out with her left hand to take his hand. He does not respond. Mara blinks back tears, and in an effort to comfort herself, she starts to sing a song she remembers her mom singing to her a long time ago. Gloria Gaynor flows out of Mara accompanied by tears. Then there it is, the tell-tale high pitched tone, getting louder, preparing her for the tornado, the harbinger of death. Death is coming. Always coming. There is absolutely nothing she can do about it but watch it take everyone she loves and one day succumb to it herself.

Mara wakes to a hand squeezing hers. Her father struggles to sit up in bed. Mara stands up abruptly to help him but he puts a hand out, letting her know he will do this on his own. Once he is sitting up, he beams, or rather half of his face beams, while the other half sits stubbornly in the same slack position it had while he slept. He pats her hand. Mara throws her arms around her father's neck. He wraps his arm around her. They hold each other for a few moments until Ezekial pats Mara's back.

Mara swipes a hand over her face to catch any tears, then sits down next to her father once again. She reaches out and grabs his hand and holds it in both of hers. Mara is not sure how to look at her father. It is a struggle to look at his face, as half of him looks as she remembers him and half looks like what she imagines he will look like in death.

Ezekial asks his daughter, "How are Little Miss and Gloria?"

Mara holds her hands balled up in her lap like a child trying to hide a small bird from the prying eyes of a parent. "The girls are fine Daddy, worry about yourself."

Ezekial, seeing his daughter's distress, tries to comfort her. "M&M, how do I look?"

Mara looks away and lies. "You look fine Daddy, just fine."

Ezekial smiles as best he can. "Darlin', who knows if I will leave this hospital."

Mara bursts into tears. She throws her hands over her face because she can't stand the sight of his face in death right next to his face with a smile on it. Ezekial lets his daughter cry for a few minutes knowing how important this time will be after he passes.

When she calms down, Ezekial speaks to his daughter, though her hands still cover her face.

"You know M&M, death is not sadness. It's not some big bad coming to get me or you. It is simply the end of our journey here. The thought of the end is frightening, but for me, your mom is waiting on the other side. Hopefully anyway. I guess I'll see." Ezekial chuckles to himself.

Mara thinks to herself, *But Daddy I'm falling through the air and I am looking at the ground I am hurtling toward, that you will hit any second, and I am scared.*

A fatigue comes over Ezekial. He sighs and seems to be getting visibly smaller. Shrinking into himself.

"M&M, I'm tired. I think I'll close my eyes for a bit. Go home Dove, come back tomorrow."

Mara puts his hand back on the folded over lip of blanket and sheet. Then she helps him adjust until he is comfortable enough to sleep. Ezekial closes his eyes. Mara sits back down at his side, watching.

Later that night, Mara sits on the side of her bed. The fear is still with her. The feeling that everything is temporary. That she is alone, her existence tenuous. The galloping sound of her heart sounds like thunder in her ears. She closes her eyes and breathes counting to four. The tears come and she allows them. This moment she knows she is alone is the truth. Of course it is.

When the tears subside, Mara takes a few more breaths until her body no longer shudders under the truth. She opens her eyes, and standing in the doorway in front of her is Dai, his hands stuffed into his pockets. He clears his throat, which she knows he does when he is uncomfortable or unsure. Dai takes his hands out of his pockets and walks toward her with his hands balled up at his sides. As he approaches her, he opens and closes them as if to remind himself not to ball them up. He stops in front of Mara.

Mara reaches up and grabs each of his hands. She curls them both back into a ball and kisses each, as if to tell him she will love him no matter what. He sits beside her, his hands still clenched into fists and extended in front of him, wrists up, as if he is unsure what to do with them.

"I'm supposed to be comforting you, Mara."

Mara smiles to herself, gets up, and squats in front of him. She opens both of his hands from their clenched position and kisses each palm. She looks up into his eyes.

"Dai, this moment is everything, and that scares the shit out of me."

Dai pulls Mara up and onto his lap. Mara can see his scar, a smile carved into his throat. She looks away. Dai takes her arms and wraps them around his neck, then puts his hands on either side of her face.

He looks into her eyes and whispers, "If we must fall, let it be together."

Then they are falling back. His arms wrapped around Mara. Mara's arms wrapped under Dai's shoulder and her hands clinging to the top of them. By the time Dai's back hits the bed, they are clinging to each other for dear life.

Pomegranate

Jamie remembers very little about the night his little sister was born. Most of it was snapshots, lightning flash images that were half memory and half story, passed down by his dad, his grandma, his mother. Certain things had been told to him so often they had become his. It had rained like the devil, for hours, for days, they said. The power had gone out, they said. You were so excited, you drew picture after picture of you and your new little sister, they said.

What Jamie knows he remembers was the screaming, the terrible, terrifying, animal sound of his mother in pain. Her groans ripped through the tense silence of the house, at odds with the dim, flickering light of the candles and the warm-sweet of his mother's incense; things he associated with peace and calm, with his mother's low, chanting voice as she pressed oiled hands into the pressure points of his feet, swept light hands over his legs, his arms. There was nothing calm about his mother now. He may have only been five, but even he knew something big was happening on the other side of the closed living room door. Every so often he'd hear a voice, his father's, the doula's, at once calm and also so very obviously scared and then their voices would be swallowed again by his mother's screams.

Jamie's grandma had been with him in his bedroom, he remembers, distractedly telling him stories, one eye on the door. The yells from the living room went on and on. His grandmother winced with each one. Every so often she would rise as if compelled by some force too big for Jamie to understand, even as he witnessed it. It was as if she was being pulled, some link tugging tight, reeling her in but she always hesitated at the threshold of the living room, paused, just for a moment and then the screams would die down for a little bit and she would relax back onto the bed with Jamie, open the book back up and start reading from the same page again. The giant repeated his "fee fi fo fum" line at least ten times, Jamie remembers.

Finally, his mother's howling took on a tone and decibel that made Jamie cover his ears. One scream seemed to go on forever. It was endless. Jamie thought his mother would be screaming for eternity.

And then it stopped.

And then there was silence.

His grandma had given up the story once again and was gripping his arm too tightly, her nails digging into his skin. Her whole body strained toward the living room, toward whatever was happening behind the door. Jamie strained too, to hear, the silence suddenly oppressive and unnatural after so much noise. They listened and listened and listened until at last, there was a noise, a teeny, tiny noise, like a kitten or a puppy, an ancient noise of something little and hungry.

Jamie's grandma released his arm and fell back onto the bed. He turned to ask her if it was all over and was embarrassed to see tears running down her face. He'd never seen a grownup cry before. He hadn't known it was possible. He looked away.

And then it's the flashbang memories again, grenades that explode in his mind if he thinks about them, all high contrast and vibrant but not his. You went running into the living room, they said. You kissed your mother on the cheek, they said. You held your little sister, they said. There's proof of the last in a photo, a Polaroid, blue tacked alongside his pictures on the fridge. In the white rectangle at the bottom, someone had written Jamie and Carissa, 1995 XX.

He must have fallen asleep on the sofa because he remembers waking up, in his bed now, the house suddenly silent, dark.

Jamie went in search of water, making his way to the kitchen through the darkened hallways. Once upon a time, he had been afraid of the dark, of the things that liked to live in the dark. "But," his mother had explained, "those things don't exist. They're only fairy stories."

And anyway, even if he was still a little bit scared, he could see lights coming from the kitchen.

This part of the night, Jamie remembers with crystal clear clarity, despite his father insisting Jamie must have seen it in a film, dreamt it. Jamie knows deep in his bones, the way he knows his own name, that this memory was his, not something he had inherited or created out of a mish-mash of horror films and fairy tales.

The lights had been low, Jamie remembered, the electricity still out. He had been expecting his dad or his grandma in the kitchen and was surprised to find his mother standing at the counter.

She was slicing something up, something red and juicy. She hadn't seen him at first, too focused on what she was doing. Jamie can still see his mother, as he had seen her then, towering, powerful, her hair a dark wave of braids, interrupted every so often with the shine of a gold jewel, falling over her shoulders and down her back. She looked so strong, he remembered thinking, so capable, he knew he was safe with her, in their ring of light cast by the candles. As Jamie watched, she brought a piece of whatever she was cutting into, to her mouth, sucking it down, licking her fingers free of juice. Jamie remembered then, the picnic they'd had just a few days ago before the rain had started, before his little sister had started to come. He remembered the chill of his freshly squeezed OJ, the satisfying crisp-crunch of his watermelon.

And he remembered the pomegranates.

He remembered the way the juice had run down his fingers, down his arms, the little pink gems popping as he plucked them from their tough rind. His mother must have saved a few because that same juice ran down her fingers now, down her arm, and dripped to the floor, where they landed in a pink splat on the linoleum. Jamie remembers tugging on his mother's nightgown, wanting her to share some of her treat. When she turned he saw the pomegranate juice had spilled down her lips, her mouth, her chin, down her crisp white nightgown, staining it red from her neckline all the way down to her belly and when he looked he saw juice bleeding all over the counter, up the back wall, dripping down onto the cabinet fronts below. His mother would have shouted at him if he'd messed his clothes in such a way, if he'd dirtied the kitchen like that, but now she only smiled, seemingly unsurprised to see him there.

"My sweet baby boy," his mother said. The sight of her red-stained teeth made something recoil inside of himself. His heart thumped in his chest, rattling his ribs as if it wanted an escape. The lights seemed suddenly very low, enhancing the shadows in the dark corners instead of lessening them. He was scared, he realized, truly scared for the first time since his mother had said there were no monsters. For the first time in his life, Jamie questioned his mother. He questioned whether she wasn't one of the very monsters he should be afraid of with her blood-red teeth grinning down at him.

"My sweet baby boy," she said again, stroking a stained finger down his cheek. They smelled raw, like uncooked meat, and Jamie's stomach turned.

"Here," she said, "eat this. It's good for you. It'll make you strong."

She held out a piece of pomegranate.

"Open," she ordered, holding the fruit up to his lips. He didn't want to, but the bright of his mother's eyes compelled him. He opened his mouth. His mother fed him the piece of pomegranate. It tasted strange, almost but not quite like the pomegranates they'd eaten a few days ago. It tasted like pennies, the flavor bright and sharp. There was a sweetness, but not of fruit. Jamie was reminded of the time he'd fallen and his tooth had been knocked out, this same sharp-sweet filling his mouth. It tasted like life. He felt it land in his stomach. He wanted to spit but didn't want to risk his mother's wrath despite the mess she'd made of the kitchen.

"Good boy," his mother murmured, turning back to the counter and picking up a piece for herself. She swallowed like an albatross, without chewing and hummed in satisfaction.

Jamie had gone back to bed without his water. He'd laid down. Closed his eyes. The last image he remembered seeing before he was taken by sleep was of the pomegranate, the juice running down the cupboard door, splashed up the wall and down his mother. He smacked his lips, and the taste in his mouth flashed back to life, lingering on his tongue. Jamie compared the flavor in his mouth to the pomegranates he'd eaten before and wondered. Sleep was rushing up to claim him, but he wondered, in those last seconds, why his mother was up, eating pomegranates in the kitchen in the middle of the night, in the dark, he wondered why they were different, why the pomegranate he'd eaten at the picnic was bright-sharp and the one he'd eaten in the kitchen was copper-sweet. Lastly, he wondered if what his mother had fed him was even pomegranate at all.

That was the last thing Jamie remembered from the night his little sister was born because then, with the tang of his mother's pomegranate still fresh on his tongue, Jamie slept.

Mr. Landry

I sat on my porch with a glass of sweet limeade in one hand and Philibert, my kitty cat, in my lap and watched the world beyond my little
white fence. I do not care to go beyond my fence; I usually enjoy being
as alone as I am. But sometimes I do fancy bringing the world to me
when feeling especially alone, and this was one of those days.

It was a fine day, just like the weather man said, with big bright
white puffy clouds floating over the softly rolling emerald grass dotted
with spicy autumn sage. Hot and smothering like always. Behind my
house, a one-story Creole cottage my daddy built but that I painted
myself in 1967, I heard the sparrows, the warblers in the oaks and ma-
ples, with the grass mice scurrying through the bushes. Flies and
mosquitoes were buzzing in my ear, around the veranda, and I swatted
them with my newspaper fan. Philibert was purring in my arms as I
stroked his velvet ears. I did a little jig in my seat when I heard a tune
from Boozoo Chavis come on the radio beside me. Now you may not
know a thing about Boozoo Chavis, but let me tell you that he was the
bees' knees back when I was a young fellow. Zydeco was the wind, and
boy did we float.

I thought I heard some poor baby crying in the distance, but it was
not a baby. My neighbor, Cecilia Turner, and her crazy dog both yap-
ping over my fence and through the row of pink magnolia trees that sat
between our lands:

"Philippe!" she yelled. "Mr. Philippe! Where you at?"

Cecilia was old enough to be my mama and I'm old as dirt, about
half-a-century and some odd years. We were distant cousins, as everyone here was blood and kin, and I treated her as such, going over to the
fence to entertain her chitchat and ask her about her son.

Our properties were right next to each other, but separated from
the rest of the town. Our families owned most of the good fertile land
on the outskirts. Everyone else lived in the eastern marshes and we
were lucky enough to have land that was flat and fertile, with green

grass and lovely wild flowers like ours.

Miss Cecilia *was* like my mama in a way, always pulling out and bringing over pecan candies, jars of jam, baskets of bread. I loved when she happened to have extra fresh shrimps and crawfish, always warning, "Cook these right fast, now. I been keeping them, so they ready to just rot." I supposed she had to be this vigilant, with a grown live-in son like Herbert.

Herbert was forty-years-old but lacked all the sense to make something out of having a good mama. He went with all those other poor boys to Vietnam. Some of our boys didn't make it back. Others came back without legs, arms, or eyes. Poor Herbert came back without any brains. I saw the pictures of what the Vietcong did to our soldiers on the television, so I knew that being around all that killing and shooting must have scared his brains clear out of his head. But brains or no brains, I tried to stay away from Herbert. His eyes always looked as if he had just woken up, sucked up and dry.

"Did you hear about Greta's boy?" Cecilia asked me once I reached our shared fence.

"No, no I haven't heard a thing," I replied. "What's going on?"

Greta used to be an ugly woman. But she had two fine-looking boys. They lived in the marshes and Greta cleaned houses in the city. There wasn't a father around, which was usual with their kind. Last I heard of her was that she took one of her tennis shoes and beat her smaller boy in the face and mouth when he gave her backtalk.

"Well, you know how she gave that little one all kinds of hickeys on the face when she beat him up? Oh, she's just as shady as the sun setting at seven-thirty, that's right. The boy had been complaining about the children teasing him for having holes in his pants and she went all into a rage."

The children teased me, too, when I was a little boy. They didn't tease me for having holey pants, for I was a well-dressed boy. My mama and daddy had enough money to build us a big house and buy my brothers and me brand new clothes and toys. I was a good boy and came from a good family, I didn't like to get dirty or hurt, so I was teased. When it rained the ragamuffins pushed me in the mud, they pulled at my trousers when the teachers were not looking, and stepped on my patent leather shoes. I wasn't too proud to cry to my mama, but she did nothing. My mama was a very busy woman, throwing soirées and passing good times.

"Well, he's all right, isn't he? Don't tell me Greta hit the boy again."

"Let me finish now! Well, the older one wanted to get his brother some good clothes. So, he takes himself to the gambling house in St. Bernard's Parish, you know, the Alligator House...just awful, I know! That was two nights ago..."

I heard Philibert calling me and I turned to see him on the porch, his neck outstretched, refusing to step down the veranda steps. Philibert was so needy when I wasn't holding him.

"Just wait! I'm speaking with Miss Cecilia."

Philibert stepped back as if offended and walked in a circle until he settled on his paws to spy on me.

"That damn cat of yours...well, I'll finish up so you can get back. Well, he got smacked up real good when he got back, just all beat up! And he's a good-looking boy!"

She looked at me to respond or agree with her and when I didn't she waved her hand and continued, but I was so damn hot I didn't feel like playing gossip buddy this afternoon. My feet ached to sit back down on my porch with my limeade.

"Well, it's gotten real bad over there, be careful, now. I hope I never have to go that way, no sir... not me. And these children nowadays never listen when somebody tells them to do..."

Cecilia talked just as much as my wife did when she got into a hissy fit. Talked about this and that and I would just nod and pretend to listen, when in reality I was reading the paper or fixing me a whiskey or Bourbon. I especially enjoyed Bourbon when Suzette would talk me to death, but now in my loneliness I longed to have a conversation partner in my house.

I remembered the day Suzette left with my children, but not like how I should have remembered.

"I'm hitting the door and never coming back!" she had declared. She materialized out of thin air before me with two packed suitcases and our four handsome children, also holding suitcases. All four frowning in a row, and all I could think of was why were the children dressed in their coats so damn early in the morning.

I remembered very little of that night, slouched in my great-grandfather's chair, as I happened to have overdosed on my whiskey.

I do remember my boy, though.

My youngest and only boy, he was about seven-years-old when Suzette took him and the other children. My daughters were always sashaying around like their mother but my boy stayed close, sitting with me on the porch, struck by the wind chimes and the animals that scurried around the property. He was the only child that Suzette let me name, even though he favored her the most, but most of the children favored Suzette by the grace of the Holy Father. But she spat him out. Lean and small-boned – he would be tall – with wavy sandy blond hair and skin the color of sugar cookies made with brown sugar. He was a beautiful boy and I wonder if he grew up to be a gentleman.

When Suzette left, she took the Oldsmobile and I never found the time to buy a new one. No need to do that anyway. I walked to where I needed to go when I was younger. Not that I'm too old or anything, but knees need rest, so I pay Herbert to make my groceries and run errands.

When Cecilia finished her rant, I pardoned myself and went back to my veranda. Seeing her reminded me of the new bottle of brandy that Herbert bought me for mending his wrist. After polishing off the limeade, I went to the kitchen and fixed a glass of it.

Philibert looked a little parched, rubbing against my leg, so I fixed him some ice water in his dish. Then I thought he would be hungry so I put a little broiled catfish in his bowl. Philibert often got sleepy after he ate so I fixed him a little cot with a pillow next to his cat dish so he wouldn't have to travel very far to sleep.

I sat back on my porch and took two big swigs of my brandy, looking out beyond my big field of grass and fence. Boy it was hot and I felt a little bothered by my shirt, but I didn't dare remove it. I wouldn't want to scare all the little boys and girls that were running around on the grass and nearby road.

I took out a cigarette, lit it, sat back, and tuned into my radio. My smoking annoyed Philibert, so it was good he was inside the house. The radio man was interviewing a woman, a mother of one of the astronauts who died when that shuttle exploded. Poor lady, I wish the media people would leave those families alone.

My skin prickled when I looked out into the distance and spotted one of the town boys walking down the sidewalk hitting my fence with a tree branch. Roland, a nice boy who lived close by who lived with his mother, Inez, a pretty lady who worked at the post office. Her sister was my nephew's wife's cousin, so I tried to look out for kin, as long as it was from my porch.

I always saw Roland when he walked to school in the mornings and from school in afternoons, alone and carrying all his books in his hand. He dressed well too, even if he wore his pants like all the kids, loose and baggy like a porter. He always had the nicest wool sweaters and cotton shirts, with nice clean shoes. I also saw him when he walked with his cronies, a group of tall and young men just as handsome with muscled arms. I smiled when I saw those boys who laughed and shoved each other because I never had friends like that. And when I heard Roland carrying groceries from the store, I would look out my window to make sure he passed by in one piece. He was a strong boy and those muscles sure did come in handy, being the only man in his house.

"Come on over here, boy!" I called out, waving my hand in the air.

Roland smiled a little and proceeded to open my fence and walk up my pathway. He wore a snow-white shirt with pressed jeans, and his dark skin sort of glistened in the sun, sweating a little.

"Good afternoon, Mr. Landry," he said, standing before my veranda. "How you doing, sir?"

He was squinting and scrunching up his face against the hot sun.

"Come on out of that sun, boy," I offered. "It can be a little hard on the eyes and you already black as the night."

Philibert walked out the house and walked down the steps to rub against Roland's legs, purring. He never walked down the porch steps, unless it was Roland. I never locked Philibert up in rooms to keep him from going outside because I never had to.

"Oh no, that's all right, sir, I got to keep moving," he replied smiling, waving his hand then using it to cover his eyes. Roland looked a lot like my son if he was much darker and older. I wondered if life would've been easier or harder for me if I looked like Roland back in my day.

"Where ya going?"

He looked down at the ground.

"I don't like to lie, sir," he said.

I smiled wider and let Philibert jump back onto my lap, stroking behind his ear.

"Don't worry, boy," I said, "I won't tell..." Then I did a little fast thinking, remembering my conversation with Cecilia. "You going to that gambling house, aren't you?"

Roland's face truly went long and he stopped chewing his gum, looking off in the direction of Cecilia's house.

"How's Ms. Turner? Is she okay after her fall?"

"Oh, she's all right. You better answer me, boy."

"Yes, sir, but I do it only for fun, sir. I don't gamble for the money, my mama would have my neck. I just hear that they have some really good card players there and nobody here is a challenge."

"Well, just go on ahead. There's no point in wasting good talent on these here slow folks. You have some fun."

The smile Roland gave me almost made me leap out of my chair. He had the whitest teeth that just seemed to shine you blind and bright eyes that leapt at you. My son used to smile at me like that when I would give him a lollipop dipped in Bourbon.

I was still in my chair stroking Philibert, glad that I was able to make this boy feel some kind of joy. I think his mama was a little hard on him.

Roland left and I watched him hurry down the sidewalk on his way to the Alligator Club. It was no place for a nice boy like that to be hanging around, but Roland could handle himself, I was sure of that. And if he couldn't handle himself, well, I would be right here on this porch. Some of us just needed a damn break.

The afternoon passed with Cecilia calling me over to the fence about four or five times, getting on my damn nerves. She knew damn well I was a little intoxicated, but insisted that I help her get a splinter out of her finger, help her move an oak table Herbert had found, and eat dinner with her.

I didn't eat dinner with her, but I made her fix me a plate, then ate it on my porch, sharing some of it with Philibert. As I ate I watched the sun disappear on my right to the West beyond the swamps, and the stars appear slowly but inevitably. The liquor eventually left my system as the evening arrived and I soon heard the crickets and owls begin their night and mating calls.

There were no streetlights in this part of town, but I spotted Roland in the darkness of the beyond. He was trying to be quiet, all sneaky-like, but I saw him, got up, and walked down the walkway to the fence, just in time to meet him at my gate.

The night grew silent all of a sudden when I saw him up close. He wasn't walking, but was dragging along, holding his thigh with a bloody hand. He had a deep gash down the side of his face that looked as if someone had took a dagger to his cheek and his lips were bloodied and smashed-looking. The clean white shirt of the day was now splotched and smeared with blood and dirt, torn down the front revealing a heaving chest. I must have scared him, walking up silently, and he jumped back raising his fists, before squinting to see who I was, then relaxing a bit.

"Put those dukes back down, boy," I said. "What happened at that gambling house?"

"Evening, sir," he replied, "I'm all right, I'll be okay."

He didn't look okay at all, so I insisted that he come inside the house. I never ever took people inside of the house, not since Suzette and the children left. But he was hurt so badly. He tried to be polite, saying that he would be fine and dandy. But I told him I would tell his mama, so he agreed. Sometimes these children, especially boys, need a little persuasion.

Inside the house, it was dark and I took him straight to the wash-room where I cleaned up his wounds. Those derelicts used dull-shaped objects, keys and rings with stones maybe, to cut him when they weren't punching him. Thank goodness, he didn't have anything broken, just bruises and ugly cuts. He was just as good as a dog, sitting still and not saying a word. He was breathing heavy and still sweating, probably from all that fighting, and it felt good on my hands and arms, just to be close to someone. He reminded me so much of my son; I almost called him by his name.

"Thank you, sir," Roland said, as I was cleaning a deep cut he had on his left arm, "but I really have to go. I told my mama that I would be in by midnight."

"Don't worry, I'll take you home," I said. "Everything will be fine. We got to get these here cuts and bruises all cleaned so you won't have ugly scars on that nice face. She would be real mad if you spoiled this here face."

He sat still and I heard his stomach growl a bit.

"You're hungry?"

He shook his head quickly and I stood up and chuckled. I really didn't want Roland to leave just yet, so I went into the kitchen and warmed up a little bowl of gumbo, also fixed him a cup of chamomile tea with some special sugar.

At the table, I ate a little but Roland didn't. He just sat there staring at the gumbo, stiff, occasionally sipping the tea. The lights were off in the house, so I don't even think he noticed me watching him in the dim dining room. It was much better than watching Philibert lick and smack out of his dish. I even got a little nervous when I realized that I should have been talking to the boy instead of just looking at him.

When he finished his tea, he sat back, real still and quiet. His neck was strong, but his head looked as if it was real heavy.

"Well, I appreciate everything, sir, but I really got to get going," he said, slowly pushing his chair back. His words were slurred and I almost couldn't understand him.

"You've been drinking, boy?" I asked him, scrunching up my eyes and nose real hard, pretending to smell alcohol on his breath.

"A little," he said. "It was free...I don't feel good."

"It's that alcohol, boy," I said, walking behind him and gently pushing his shoulders forward from the dining room down the hallway. "You a lightweight, aren't you? I could tell."

"Where we going?" he asked me. "I can't sleep here sir, I've got to-"

"Don't you worry about a thing, Roland," I said, unlocking the door to Suzette's room. "I'll explain everything to Inez tomorrow. Nobody will ever suspect you did any wrong."

I kept Suzette's room all locked up and cleaned, changing the potpourri every month or so. But it was all clean and done up for nothing. Now I smiled with all the happiness that I had someone in it after all these years. Would she be upset? No, she wasn't dead so she couldn't watch me.

I could feel Roland leaning against my hands, maybe pushing to get out of the room, maybe truly hit by the gumbo and special sugar. I laid him down on the bed, on the side that Suzette would sleep on. I think I was sweating just as much as he was now, and I felt bad for him for a short moment, thinking of how that sweat was stinging his poor wounds. His breathing was slow and laborious and he rolled onto his side, holding his head as he moved into a baby-like position.

I smiled for a moment, thinking of how he looked like my son and made me feel like my wife used to when she was pretty and happy.

I didn't want to, but I turned to go look for Philibert to go lock him up. I found him on the stove trying to get to the pot with remnants of gumbo. Spoiled brat. I snatched him and slowly walked up the stairs.

I put Philibert in one of the old guest rooms that had a big queen size bed, hoping he could sleep well. I never locked Philibert up in all the years I lived in this house. But this was a special night.

Black Barbie

Daddy straddled the heap of toys that lived on the floor of our play-room in Brentwood, Long Island. Tiny plastic arms splintered out as though bidding for a chance to accompany me to Becky Carrigan's* sleepover that night. Daddy sifted unceremoniously through water-damaged board games and the action figures that my sisters and I mostly used as our dolls' eager boyfriends. Beneath the Sega cartridges and tufts of nylon hair, Daddy unearthed a land mine. It was part of a limited edition and in an unopened, double-wide package to contain its power.

I felt a sour feeling creep to my bowels: Daddy held out a Black Barbie.

Before that moment, I would have described Becky as a nice girl, my friend. The girl who would always share her snack, the girl who generously expended all of her patience trying to teach me how to do a backflip during recess. At that moment, it became clear to me that I also saw Becky as white. I somehow knew that held a sort of reverence, and that giving her a doll that looked nothing like her was out of order. It was confusing to even me because, as it often happens, the more Khaholis moved to Brentwood, the more Beckys moved out. Somehow the thought of gifting a Black Barbie to a white girl made me feel out of place in a town where most people looked just like me.

Then I thought, just for a moment, that maybe Becky would be glad to receive this doll. After all, she didn't complain about the clothes she wore, though I considered them suitable only for sleeping and raking leaves. I was embarrassed by that thought and reminded myself that most of the kids got free lunch at school, and that 'beggars can't be choosers' could not apply to anyone living in the suburbs. It wasn't okay for me to suddenly categorize Becky to ease my nervousness. Becky deserved better than my thoughts. And goddammit, Becky deserved a white Barbie.

Daddy noticed none of my hesitation and threw Black Barbie under his arm. He thought Barbie was still the default gift for any ambitious young gal. And why not? Barbie is a doctor, after all. She has the natural temperament of a flight attendant, and her feet molded only for heels let us know that she's freak in the sheets. Oh, she's also an astronaut. But he failed to realize that Black Barbie...Barbie with an asterisk...was not a toy for every girl. She was sometimes the gift you gave to other Black girls if their parents didn't think her smiling while being dark-skinned set a bad example for their daughter. In fact, this particular Black Barbie moved to our playroom floor when a local toy store went under, so Daddy bought her nice and cheap.

Please, Daddy. Don't make me take her is what I thought.

"Thanks Daddy," is what I said.

We headed out to Becky's, but first, we stopped by the sporting goods store to buy a sleeping bag. I couldn't be the only girl at the sleepover who didn't own one.

When we arrived at Becky's, I was greeted by her mother. She wore a warm smile and a sensible brassy bob. The inside of their two-story house was tidy yet outdated; a symptom of a home without a father, I assumed. I think I remember faux wood finishing on the railing of the stairs and the wall molding, but that may be the color my memory associates with discomfort. I instinctively scanned the living room for other Black girls; girls I hoped would make me feel lighter about the gift-wrapped bomb I was carrying. There was a dark-haired, olive-skinned girl to whom I kept throwing glances, trying to figure out if she would be an ally if shit went down.

After settling in, the other guests and I sat scattered on the floor and couch, facing Becky who sat center stage on the big recliner. Becky's mom lined up all of the gifts and began handing them to Becky one by one. I eyed mine the entire time, half hoping to get it over with, and the other half hoping the four horsemen would interrupt the party. It didn't occur to me to hope that Becky would like the doll.

"This one is from...Ka...Kay-hoe-lee?" is what Becky's mom probably said when she picked up my gift, and I probably didn't correct her. Becky tore open the wrapping paper and there it was, with its suddenly ironic smile and crown.

Then, not a word.

For the longest second, the room felt both empty and stiflingly full.

Like everyone in the room had suddenly become adept at hearing the tones of silence.

Becky's mother heard guilt.

"What a beautiful doll," she managed to blurt out. She was looking right at me. Her compliment brightened the spotlight around me, but I knew then that it was better than saying nothing. The olive-skinned girl, judging by the unwarranted attitude she wielded at me that afternoon, may have had the foresight to snuff out any ethnic affiliation she may have had with me and that brazen Black Barbie. I could feel my darkness floating through the white room, contained and surrounded like a drop of oil in water.

Becky's older sister heard an alarm. One of those old-school alarms created during WWII, a throwback to the old Brentwood. Such an alarm was outdated and unnecessary, but still tested periodically in our town every so often; a horn that sounded like a vacuum cleaner with a short in its cord would blare, to remind us that there are still people on guard waiting fearlessly and hopefully for someone to dare to mutilate our ground with their footprints. Becky's sister viewed Black Barbie as an act of invasion.

Becky kept silent atop her upholstered throne and wore a look of genuine confusion, the sweetest reaction a bird-on-her-shoulder-Disney-Princess like her could muster. The next gift was handed to her, but I couldn't tell you what it was. I only looked up from my hot cloud of self-consciousness when it was finally time to go outside and play.

The fresh air popped the bubble around me almost instantaneously. I don't remember the games we played, but I do remember running and laughing the way kids do. Games were improvised, created, and distinguished with as little as a transitional word. We accepted this flow and changed together. We played until Becky's mom diverted my attention.

I remember her looking down at me and saying, "That really is a beautiful doll." She was old (to me) and slightly overweight, and probably wasn't running beside me. But in my memory, she was jogging alongside me with a smile painted on her face like streaks of camouflage. She chased me through the yard as the other children played in an imaginary world I no longer belonged to.

Still, I was eight years old, so Becky's mom was able to redeem herself with s'mores. She had gathered dry sticks, piled them into a pyramid in the backyard, and lit them with a long electric lighter. With no barrier between us and the fire, or between the fire and the grass, it all felt *wild*. We roasted marshmallows. I let the guilt melt away and replaced it with toasted saccharine and the type of best friendship that only lasts as long as a fourth-grade slumber party.

When there was more light radiating from fireflies than from the sun, we ran back into the house all gassy and giggly. I followed the other girls toward the bedrooms when Becky's sister stood in my path at the middle landing of the staircase; her arms crossed, with a facial expression that should have told me shit was about to go down after all and I was all alone.

"What are *you* doing here?"

She stood on guard. I wish I would've said something clever or at least met her glare with a more confident one, but what I remember is walking past her with heat in my face, and trying to reintegrate into the party of girls who may or may not have been thinking exactly what Becky's sister said.

I walked into Becky's room without looking back. All of her guests were sitting, standing, hanging, yelling, laughing. There were glow-in-the-dark stickers of the stars and planets on her walls and ceiling, and the open window let the freedom of summer blanket the room. We were transported to the day before, back when my Black Barbie stayed at home and the intricacies of race were only on the horizon. Even the olive-skinned girl was seduced by this nostalgia and offered to share her comforter with me.

My sleeping bag felt like an affectation I had grown out of. We hollered ourselves to sleep, and as soon as we woke up, it was time to go.

I was relieved that there was no breakfast being made, only parents being called; I feared the keen morning sun would expose some sort of wreckage. I was proud that Daddy arrived on time, the responsible Black father he showed he was. I climbed into the passenger seat of our white minivan and shut the door, hoping to escape the exhaustion of blackness.

"How was the party?" Daddy asked.

"Good," I said.

Becky's family moved away from Brentwood soon after.

I imagine her packing up her wardrobe made up of sweatpants, long t-shirts, and a pair of white Keds. I imagine eight-year-old Becky walking away from me, followed by long wavy hair, streaked with the same iridescent gold as the skin of a marshmallow peep.

I imagine that the Carrigans made it to one of the neighboring towns, a place where there were no Khaholis but plenty of tennis courts, where people would look at her t-shirt with the peeling letters of some family reunion or company slogan, and pause before saying, "That really is beautiful."

I hope she brought Black Barbie with her.

Last name changed for privacy.

Little Brother

"I'm worried about my brother," my mother says softly. My four-year-old son, Michael, breathes her a quick "Hi Nana!" and rushes over to the living room to build yet another fort. I settle in and pour myself a cup of tea, staring at my mother, waiting. Her face is fixed between tears and defiance. She has the broken heart of one who empathizes with everyone she meets - a feeler, a woman who knows. She knows your pain before you even know it yourself, a valuable trait for a registered nurse. But today the pain is hers, intertwined with her baby brother's, twists of sorrow suffocating each heart even though they are an entire continent away.

"He's coughing up blood," she says.

"What? Why?"

"It could be pneumonia or tuberculosis, but given his history, it's probably stage four lung cancer," she tells me. "You know he's an alcoholic, right?"

My mother always tells me this as if it is news. As if I'd never noticed the permanent stench of days old rum on my uncle's skin, or the constant zigzag of his gait. As if his thickly slurred accent was undetectable by anyone other than his parents or siblings.

My Uncle Mikey shares the title of "Alcoholic" along with nearly every other male in my mother's large family. I cannot recall seeing my grandfather sober, and remember it being standard protocol to lock up the liquor cabinet whenever he came to visit. If there is a gene that indicates addiction, my mother's family is cursed with it. Of the three boys, Mikey suffered the most, yet to my mom, he was the sweetest of them all. When Grampy died a year or so after Grammy, Mikey took over the home that he and his ten siblings grew up in. He would welcome stray friends into the small, pastel green stucco rancher, feeding them what he could and giving them space to rest for as long as they needed.

"He's such a good, good person," my mom sighs. "You know, his best friend, Huey, he died last week – he was really sick. Mikey tried to resuscitate him, but he died anyway. They were as close as brothers. It must have been so hard on him to watch his friend die in his arms like that."

My mom moves over to the low backed stools, the same dark mahogany carefully chosen to match the table and cupboards in the large open kitchen. Uniformity is my mother's addiction. Things need to match and flow. They need to be clean.

"I called him a couple of days ago to check in on him," she says as she draws her tea closer, sliding it along the cold granite island. "He told me he had been sick for a week. Coughing up blood for a week," she says, shaking her head. "I told him to get himself to the hospital immediately, or I would fly down there and take him myself. He still didn't go. A neighbor called an ambulance for him yesterday. He was coughing up so much blood and vomiting it up too."

Coughing up blood is never good, but I know enough to know that vomiting up blood is a terrible sign. There is no need to ask. My mom's worried brow betrays her thoughts – her little brother is dying.

Being so far from home has always had its challenges for my mom, but the worst of them all is in not being able to get to her loved ones in haste when they are sick. Traveling to the Bahamas takes a half day at least, and of course, there's the cost. Not knowing what is happening with Mikey is a cruel form of self-inflicted torture. We either distract ourselves or wait impatiently by the phone. Of course, we opt for distraction and head out of the house. My mother needs to pick up a faux fireplace she has recently purchased and requires some extra muscle to get it in and out of her car. It's as good enough of a distraction as any.

As we roll through the minutes and hours of the day, I begin to forget that my uncle is even sick. My mother and I are enjoying each other's company, and even sharing some laughs over The Home Depot employee who is the spitting image of my own little brother. At least, we think he is; and so we ask to take his picture for proof.

Back at the house, I take down the usual order for dinner. Prawn tempura, chicken karage, miso soup, spicy tuna roll. Takeout sushi is in constant rotation at my parents' house. We never seem to grow tired of it, despite culturally being the furthest thing from Japanese you could imagine. Our Caribbean relatives have always thought us a bit strange for thriving on tobiko and seaweed.

My sister, Jina, arrives just in time and sets a spot for herself next to me at the kitchen table. Michael chews away at battered pieces of chicken while we marvel over the existence of my brother's doppelgänger, and for a moment, we all forget about my uncle.

After dinner, my sister and I head outside to bring the fireplace into the one-bedroom suite downstairs, while Michael runs back to his fort and my father sits transfixed by CNN.

The fireplace is not small or light, but it's manageable, and Jina and I work quickly to get it inside. We ease it through the door, resting it along the wall in front of the burgundy loveseat where my mother sits waiting for us. It's off-center, but for now, and in a rare moment, she doesn't seem to mind. I plug it in and hit the power button. Orange and blue electric light flickers in the shape of digital flames, and we are immediately blasted with faux warmth. It is effective, if anything.

Satisfied, Jina and I make our way back up to the main floor, while our mother lingers in the warmth with her thoughts. Upstairs, Michael bounces from cushion to floor to table to cushion, fighting his late-night fatigue. I sink back into the living room couch for a few moments, fascinated by Rosie O'Donnell's tiny appearance as Betty in the 1994 remake of *The Flintstones*. I sense that my father has something to say, so I glance his way.

"Where's your mother?" he asks quietly.

"Still downstairs. Why?"

"I have to talk to her. About her brother." He stares at me, waiting for his words to sink in.

"He died," he says.

"What...what?" Only moments ago I found out that he was sick. There was still time. Time to figure out what was wrong. Time to book a flight. Time to say goodbye. "What happened? How? How, Daddy?"

My dad just shakes his head, while I shake myself into coping mode, transforming into the dutiful daughter that I am. As the eldest, I take care of things, round up the troops, make sure everyone else is okay first. Isn't that how it's supposed to be? Stunned, I walk into the kitchen to collect my thoughts. The hours before this moment have left their presence throughout the house. In my mind, our faint outlines still surround the dark mahogany table, the air still tainted with raw fish and soy sauce. Our former selves are ghosts, oblivious to the suffering that lies ahead.

I walk back downstairs, half expecting my mom to be in tears, as if somehow she already knows. But she doesn't, and part of me wants to tell her right there, but despite wearing my responsible eldest hat, with my father upstairs, it's not up to me.

"Mommy, what are you doing?"

"Just thinking about Mikey."

"Are you going to come upstairs?" I ask meekly.

"I'm coming," she sighs, her eyes glistening with tears unshed.

I head back upstairs quickly, and urge Michael to say goodnight to his Aunty Jina and Grampy.

"Time for bed, Michael – let's go."

"Okay Mommy." He springs across the last of the cushions and wraps his gangly arms around the neck of my weary father. "Good night Grampy!"

"Good night, kid. See you in the morning."

I usher Michael upstairs, hoping I can get him behind a closed door in time. Protect him from what I know is coming. I brace myself as we make our way into the spare bathroom upstairs, trying hard to focus on the sound of his bubbly chatter, of bedtime stories and cuddles and blue blanket - the priorities of innocence. I shut the door behind us, turn on the tap and wait.

In some cultures, wailing with abandonment is acceptable when mourning the loss of a loved one. I first heard my mother wail so freely at my Grammy's funeral eleven years ago. Sitting in the hot Bahamian church, I listened to my Aunt Betty let out the first tortured cry of a child abandoned by her mother. With every mention of my grandmother's name, the chorus grew louder as each of her children bound their cries together in their grief. Among them, I could hear my mother. It was a shock to the system like none I had ever felt before. Sitting with my younger brother and sister, afraid to move, I stared deftly ahead as the tears streamed down my face. Every adult I had known and looked up to had become someone else entirely in the church that day. They were still just children, after all.

My mother's wailing ceased after that day, at least as far as she would let me hear. Her tears still flowed from year to year, but she kept them silent, even through her father's funeral a year later. Only in this moment am I reminded of my mother's vulnerability; of the extent of the pain that she can feel.

As my son reaches for his flashing light toothbrush, my heart jolts as I hear the first of my mother's cries. Each wail that follows strips away at the rawness of her grief.

"Oh-oh, yellow light," exclaims Michael through a mouthful of toothpaste.

I grin at my son through the tears welling up in my eyes. I let the water run as he proudly shows me how he can brush all of his teeth before the red light glows.

"Look Mommy, look," he announces, "all done."

"Yes Michael, you did it." I force my mouth into a loving smile. So this is what it is, to be brave for your child. Be the mother, the daughter, and the caregiver all at once. Smile through the pain and be strong. Just be strong. I continue to pray that my son won't hear his Nana in such distress, while downstairs, the dining table ghosts cover their ears as they fade into a place that will no longer exist.

We Are The Champions

Put one foot on the toilet bowl. Try to pee in a steady stream over a short white stick. Pay careful attention not to oversaturate. Remember that you are not equipped with the proper aiming tools, so getting everything into the toilet will be a dance. Gag at the smell of your pee. Follow your teeth with your tongue. Taste the chalky film in your mouth. Throw the stick into the sink when you lose balance. Keep your underwear above your knees. Extend backwards for toilet paper and wipe the seat after finishing with yourself. Sit on the seat for a while. Hold your head between your legs and say the alphabet backwards. Start over a lot to buy yourself extra time. Control a dry heave by biting down on the inside of your gums. It's time. Take careful strides to fix yourself. No underwear sticking out of your jeans. No toilet paper on your shoes. Peep into the sink. Pretend you are nonchalant. Wrap the stick in tissue and wash your hands. Then wash your face. Get enough water into your eyes that you can't tell where the tears end or begin. Dry your face. Rub harder and harder and harder. There is nothing there. Rub the nothing away. Bite down on your inner cheeks. Try to puncture the walls of your mouth. Try to taste blood and not metallic chalk.

Let weeks go by. You have finally saved enough money for the procedure. He knows and does a great job of pretending to care. When he says that he is saving up to help pay half, shake your head *yes*, and pretend to say thank you. No need to say much more. When he calls you up to ask if you need a ride to the clinic, press ignore. When he calls back to back, take the battery out of your phone.

Catch the early bus. Ignore the advertisement offering help with adoption. Ignore the smiling kid sitting in the seat next to you. When he turns to share a piece of his banana, put your headphones in. Turn up *Bohemian Rhapsody*. We are the champions my friends and we'll keep on fighting till the end. Yes, we are the champions. We are the champions. When the kid reaches for your hand, look out the window.

Notice your reflection. Your unruly hair is unruly. Your wide nose is wider. Your brown skin is blotchy.

When you get off the bus, open your mouth so the crisp air can dry out the pre-vomit spit. Notice the signs and chanters. Be prepared to walk through a storm of pro-life protesters. Avoid eye contact. Don't look at the picket signs with bloody dead embryos. Don't look at the overweight woman pumping her Bible-bearing fists. Don't look at the balding white guy throwing pamphlets. They are not talking to you when they scream, "Murderer...Murderer!" Let a security guard in a bright yellow vest walk you through the crowd. Notice that he smells like boiled meat. Notice his hair is greasy. Notice it sticks to the sides of his head and makes little s-curls on top of the rolls in his neck. Follow him. He is your knight in shining armor.

Sit through your consultation meeting. Shake your head *yes*: you know the risks. Shake your head *no*: you are not being coerced. *Yes. No. Yes. No.* Play Sudoku until your name is called. 1, 2, 3, 4, 5, 6, 7, 8, 9.

It's your turn. When the doctor says, "Don't try to close your legs now," let your bottom half wriggle as he removes the sheet covering your thighs. Wish you were asleep. Pretend to be asleep. Roll your eyes into the back of your head and hum a medley. Any medley, it doesn't matter. Don't be surprised when *We Are the Champions* pops into your head. Go with it.

When the doctor says, "You ladies kill me with that humming. Stop being a baby," be grateful that his heavy accent is burying the English. Thank goodness you don't understand him. If you look up, he will avoid eye contact. Return to the whitewashed walls.

Remember Queen. Remember the champions. There's no time for losers. Aren't you a champion?

When a young woman about your age and build grabs your left leg and holds it in place, listen to her when she says, "Stay still." She will lean in closer and whisper, "He doesn't mean it. It's just a cultural thing." She's lying.

When muttering and growling comes from the angry doctor prepping a needle in the corner, hum that part, *And we'll keep on fighting till the end...* This is not the end. Keep on fighting.

Whisper to the woman holding your leg, "Can you hold my hand instead?" Pretend not to hear her say no. Scoot all the way down to the bottom of the exam table and put your feet into the stirrups. Ask her, "Is this gonna hurt?" But stop yourself when the sound of the vacuum cleaner overpowers the room. Roll your eyes back. Grip the sides of your gown. Hold stiff when he shoves the supposed-to-be lubricated metal tool into your stuff. Hold stiff when he cranks it open and pokes around harder than necessary. When he sticks the needle inside of you, embrace the burning sensation.

Let your humming instinct kick in louder, *Yes, we are the champions...WE ARE THE CHAMPIOOOOOONS!*

When the doctor says, "If she screams like that again, she is out of here," scream louder. Do not kick the doctor in the face. Do not open your eyes. Do not move at all. Relax like the nurse says. Let the vacuum do its job. Let your body empty. Let the fluids drip down your thigh.

When the nurse says, "You'll be able to rest in here," follow her to a seat in a room lined with women in white robes. They are all hot off the conveyor belt. They each avoid eye contact. Some sleep. Some shiver. Some cry. They are the champions of this world. When the lady next to you crosses her body, she is praying for the champions. When she turns to you and asks if you're okay, she is sincere. Do not speak to her. Look down at your robe. Ignore her completely for a few awkward seconds. Still looking down, extend your hand and let her embrace it. Fall asleep.

Fifteen years later when you are watching the news, remember her face. Control yourself when you realize that she is testifying in a case against the doctor. Pick up the controller to turn the channel as she pleads for other women to come forward. When your husband says wait, he wants to hear more about the "quack job butcher" case, grab your daughter's baby doll, pick at the lint in its hair.

When your husband says, "This dude is charged with eight counts of murder, babe." Nod *yes*. When he says, "Can you believe that there are 46 lawsuits against him?" Nod *no*. When he questions why you are holding the baby doll so tight, laugh it off. Pretend you hear your daughter crying. Run upstairs. She's asleep. Lock yourself in the bathroom. Hold your head between your legs and say the alphabet backwards. Control a dry heave by biting down on the inside of your gums. Wash your hands. Then wash your face. Get enough water into your eyes that you can't tell where the tears end or begin. Dry your face. Rub harder and harder and harder. There is nothing there. Rub the nothing away. Bite down on your inner cheeks. Try to puncture the walls of your mouth. Remember you are a champion. This is not the end.

Bios

Khaholi Bailey is a writer of fiction and memoir. Her creative work has also been featured in FLAPPERHOUSE and Breadcrumbs. She holds a bachelor's degree in creative writing from Hunter College and lives in New York City. Follow her on Instagram @beatrix_kidd0h

Zakiah Baker is a writer residing in Southern Maryland. She earned her MFA in Creative Writing & Publishing Arts from the University of Baltimore in 2017. She has an interest in historic and generational perspectives of black girlhood and womanhood. zakiahbaker.com

rebekah blake is a Black American woman and mother. She identifies as an existentialist and loves to watch movies that make her cry or that scare her enough to keep her up at night. She enjoys reading literature that gives her goosebumps. Currently, that is Martin Buber and Toni Morrison.

K.B. Carle lives outside of Philadelphia, Pennsylvania and earned her MFA from Spalding University's Low-Residency program in Kentucky. Her stories have appeared in FlashBack Fiction, Lost Balloon, former-cactus, Twist in Time Literary Magazine, Milk Candy Review, and elsewhere. She can be found online at kbcarle.wordpress.com or on Twitter @kbcarle

Jeannine A. Cook writes about the complex intersections of motherhood, activism, and the arts. Her pieces are featured in several publications including Mothering Magazine, Girl God, Mahogany Baby, Good Mother Project, and Printworks.

Cassandra Eddington is a writer and artist living in the Bronx and originally from San Antonio, TX. She received her B.A. from Wellesley College where she studied postcolonial literature and creative writing.

She received her MFA (Fiction) from Hunter College in 2018. Follow her on Instagram @cssndrah

Johannah Fienburgh is a London based, BAME writer and artist. Her writing reflects her experiences growing up in a sprawling, multi-cultured city; as such it is eclectic, vibrant and spans genres, from romance to historical to horror to sci-fi. She shares her work mainly on Instagram @johannahmf

Janyce Denise Glasper, AfroVeganChick creator, is a Philadelphia based multidisciplinary artist and writer. In addition to painting, drawing, and printmaking, she is an avid film lover, book reader, and a current contributor for The Artblog. She just finished her first novel.

Marissa Joy Leotaud is a writer and television professional. She lives in Denver, CO with her two sons.

devorah major is a California based, Caribbean focused poet and fiction writer with two novels, several short stories, various creative non-fiction essays and five books of poetry published. Her fiction ranges from magic realism to speculative fiction to realism. For more info, visit devorahmajor.com

Zuri H. Scrivens is a writer of poetry, memoir and a dash of fiction. With a passion for raw and honest writing that unearths brave perspectives, her work has appeared in The Writers' Studio's Emerge 15 and Caitlin Press' Boobs: Women Explore What It Means To Have Breasts. Instagram @zuriwriting

Vanessa Taylor is a writer currently based in Philadelphia, although the Midwest will always be home. She has work in outlets such as Teen Vogue, Racked, and Catapult. Her work focuses on exploring Black Muslim womanhood and the taboo. Follow her across social media at @bacontribe

Janelle M. Williams received her BA from Howard University and her MFA in Creative Writing from Manhattanville College. She was a 2017 Kimbilio Fiction Fellow. Her work has appeared in Kweli, Vol. 1

Brooklyn, SmokeLong Quarterly, Lunch Ticket, Auburn Avenue, The Feminist Wire, and elsewhere. She tweets @Janelleonrecord

Akilah Wise is a Los Angeles native based in Atlanta, Georgia. She is a graduate of Stanford University and the University of Michigan and is a public health researcher by training. She is currently exploring ways to meld her passion for fiction writing with her love for exploring health.

About The Editor

Ianna A. Small is the founder of midnight & indigo Publishing and creator of midnight & indigo, a literary platform dedicated to short stories and narrative essays by Black women writers. m&i is her love letter to Black women like herself, who long to reach the pinnacle of their purpose.

A media marketing executive, Ms. Small has 20+ years of experience developing partnerships, distribution and content marketing initiatives for entertainment brands including BET, Disney Channel, ESPN, ABC, FX, VH1, MTV, HOT97, and more. As the executive editor of midnight & indigo, she oversees editorial and creative direction for the digital and print platforms.

An avid fan of Black and South Asian literature, British television, and all things Jesus + The Golden Girls + Michelle Obama, she dreams of one day running midnight & indigo from a lounge chair overlooking the archipelagos of Santorini.

Ms. Small is a proud graduate of Syracuse University, daughter to Nadia, and mother of an amazing son, Jalen Anthony, who is simply: her reason.

Made in the USA
San Bernardino, CA
14 July 2020